COURTNEY MILAN

the Governess Affair

a novella

Courtney Milan: The Governess Affair

For Amy, Tessa, and Leigh.
I'm never "scared" with you all around.

Chapter One

London, October, 1835.

THE DOOR TO THE UPSTAIRS LIBRARY slammed viciously, rattling in its frame. Heavy steps marched across the room, bearing down on Hugo's desk. Fists slammed against the wood surface.

"Damn it, Marshall. I need you to fix this."

Despite that dramatic production, Hugo Marshall did not look up from the books. Instead he waited silently, listening to boots marking a path upon the carpet. He wasn't a servant; he refused to be treated as one.

After a moment, his patience was rewarded. "Fix it, *please*," the Duke of Clermont muttered.

Hugo raised his head. An untutored observer would focus on the Duke of Clermont, apparently in full command, resplendent in a waistcoat so shot with gold thread that it almost hurt the eyes. This observer would dismiss the drab Mr. Marshall, arrayed as he was in clothing spanning the spectrum from brown to browner.

The comparison wouldn't stop at clothing. The duke was respectably bulky without running to fat; his patrician features were sharp and aristocratic. He had mobile, ice-blue eyes that seemed to take in everything. Compared with Hugo's own unprepossessing expression and sandy brown hair, the untutored observer would have concluded that the duke was in charge.

The untutored observer, Hugo thought, was an idiot.

Hugo set his pen down. "I wasn't aware there was anything in need of fixing." Except the matter of Her Grace. "Anything within my purview, that is."

Clermont positively bristled with an edgy nervousness. He rubbed his nose in a manner that was decidedly unmannered. "There's something else. It's come up just this morning." He glanced out the window, and his frown grew.

The library in Clermont's London home was two floors off the ground, and claimed an uninspiring view. There was nothing to see out the window but a Mayfair square. Autumn had turned green leaves to brown and yellow.

A small bit of fading grass and a few dingy shrubberies ringed a wrought-iron bench, upon which a woman was seated. Her face was occluded by a wide-brimmed bonnet decorated with a thin pink ribbon.

Clermont clenched his hands. Hugo could almost hear the grinding of his teeth.

But his words were casual. "So, if I refuse to pander to the duchess's ridiculous demands, you'd still work everything out, wouldn't you?"

Hugo gave him a stern look. "Don't even consider it, Your Grace. You know what's at stake."

The other man folded his arms in denial. His Grace really *didn't* understand the situation; that was the problem. He was a duke, and dukes had no notion of economization. Were it not for Hugo, Clermont's vast estates would have collapsed years before under the weight of his debt. As it was, the books barely balanced—and they only did that because of the man's recent marriage.

"But she's so unamusing," Clermont protested.

"Yes, and a fine joke it will be to have your unentailed property repossessed. Convince your duchess that she well and truly wishes you back in her life. After that, you may laugh all you wish, Your Grace."

There had been money up front in the marriage settlement. But that had disappeared quickly, paying off lingering mortgages and troubling debts. The remainder of the duchess's substantial dowry had been tied up in trust by the girl's father—the funds to be released on a regular schedule, so long as the duke kept his wife happy.

Alas. The duchess had decamped four months ago.

Clermont pouted. There was no other word for it; his shoulders slumped and he kicked at the edge of the carpet like a petulant child. "And here I thought all my money worries were over. What do I hire you for, if not to—"

"All your money worries *were* over, Your Grace." Hugo drummed his fingers on the table. "And how many times must I remind you? You don't hire me. If you hired me, you'd pay me wages."

Hugo knew too much about the duke's prospects to accept anything so futile as a promise of salary. Salaries could be delayed; *wagers,* on the other hand, sanctified by the betting book at White's, were inviolable.

"Yes," the duke groused, "and about that. You said that all I had to do was find an heiress and say whatever it took to make her happy." He scowled at the carpet underfoot. "I did. Now look where it's got me—every shrewish bitch in the world thinks it her right to harp at me, over and over. When will it end?"

Hugo raised his head and looked Clermont in the eyes. It didn't take long—just a few seconds of an intent stare—and the man dropped his chin and looked away, as if *he* were the employee and Hugo his master.

It was embarrassing. A duke should have known how to take charge. But no; Clermont was so used to having others bow before his title that he'd never learned to command by force of personality.

"There appears to have been a miscommunication." Hugo steepled his fingers. "I never told you to *say* whatever it took to make her happy."

"You did! You said—"

"I told you to *do* whatever it took to make her happy."

Sometimes, Clermont was like a little child—as if nobody had ever taught him right from wrong. At this, he wrinkled up his nose. "What's the difference?"

"What you *said* was that you'd love her forever. What you actually did was marry her and take up with an opera singer three weeks later. You knew you had to keep that girl happy. What were you thinking?"

"I bought her a bracelet when she complained! How was I supposed to know she wanted fidelity from me?"

Hugo focused on the papers on his desk. Even his own late, unlamented father had managed fidelity: sixteen children worth of it, to be precise. But this was no time to remind the duke of his wedding vows. He sighed.

"Win her back," he said softly. It was his future at stake, too. After all, he wasn't an employee, receiving a salary for his hard work. He operated on a form of commission—on wagers, to be exact, in the language of the financially incompetent duke. If he brought the duke through the end of this year in one piece, he'd win five hundred pounds. That wasn't just money; those five hundred pounds would be the means to begin his own empire.

He'd worked three years on that hope. When he considered, briefly, the possibility that he might *lose*... He could almost see the shadowy figure of his father standing over him. *You bloody useless git. You'll never be anybody.*

He shook his head, sending those darker thoughts scattering. He wasn't going to be just *anybody*. He was going to be the wealthiest coal miner's son in all of England.

But Clermont wasn't meeting his eyes. Instead, he frowned and looked out the window. "It's not quite so simple."

That woman was still sitting on the bench. She'd turned her head to the side, and Hugo caught a glimpse of profile—snub nose, a smudge of pink for her lips.

"You see," Clermont muttered, "there was this governess."

Hugo rolled his eyes. Any confession that started thus could not end well.

Clermont gestured. "It happened over the summer, when I was seeing to business at Wolverton Hall."

Hugo translated this mentally: The duke had been drinking himself silly with his useless friends after his wife had flounced off and his father-in-law had tied off the once-generous purse strings. But no point in insisting on honesty from the man. He'd never get it.

"In any event," Clermont said, pointing to the bench outside, "that's her, now. Waiting. Demanding compensation from me."

"Your pardon?" Hugo shook his head in confusion.

The duke huffed. "Must I spell it out? She wants things from me."

Had he thought the duke a child? An infant, more like. Hugo kept his voice calm. "Between seeing to business at Wolverton Hall and a governess waiting outside your home demanding compensation, there are a great many events missing. For what is she demanding compensation? Who brought this matter to your attention?"

"She caught me just now, when I was returning from…well, never mind where I was," the duke said. "She was on the street, waiting for the carriage to arrive."

"And what does she want?" Hugo persisted.

Clermont gave an unconvincing laugh. "Nothing! Nothing, really. I, uh, at Wolverton Hall, I saw that she was good with the younger children. So I offered her a position taking care of my son."

"Your as-yet-unborn child."

"Yes," Clermont mumbled. "Exactly. And so she quit her position at Wolverton. And then I had no work to offer her because the duchess had left. Now she's angry, too."

The story didn't sound remotely plausible. Hugo considered, briefly, calling His Grace a liar. But it wouldn't do any good; long experience had taught him that once the duke made up a story, he'd hold to it doggedly, no matter how many holes one poked in it.

"She says she'll sit there until she receives compensation," Clermont said. "I do believe she means it. You see my dilemma. If everything works out well, I'll be bringing back the duchess in a matter of weeks. This is devilishly awkward timing. The old girl will think…"

"…That you seduced and ruined a servant?" Hugo asked dryly. That was where he would place his money.

But Clermont didn't even blush. "Right," he said. "You can see the very idea is absurd. And *of course* I did no such thing—you know that, Marshall. But matters being what they are, she needs to be gone by the time I return."

"Did you force her?" Hugo asked.

Clermont *did* flush at that. "Gad, Marshall. I'm a duke. I have no need to force women." He frowned. "What do you care anyway? They don't call you the Wolf of Clermont for your conscience."

No. They didn't. But Hugo still had one. He just tried not to remember it.

Hugo looked out the window. "Easy enough. I'll have the constables take her in for vagrancy or disturbing the peace."

"Ah…no." Clermont coughed lightly.

"No?"

"I wouldn't precisely say it was a *good* idea to put her into a courtroom. You know how they have those reporters there, writing a few lines for the papers. Someone might ask questions. She might invent stories. And while I could certainly quash any legal inquiry, what if word of this got back to Helen? You know how touchy she is on the subject of other women."

No, he wasn't getting anything useful from the man. Hugo sighed. "You talked to her. What kind of compensation does she want?"

"Fifty pounds."

"Is that all? We can—"

But Clermont shook his head. "She doesn't just want the money. I can't give her what she wants. You'll have to persuade her to go. And keep my name out of the gossip papers, will you?"

Hugo pressed his lips together in annoyance.

"After all," Clermont said, striding to the door, "it's my entire future that's at stake. When I return, I expect that you'll have sorted out this entire unfortunate affair with the governess."

It wasn't as if Hugo had any choice in the matter. His future was at stake, too, every bit as much as Clermont's. "Consider her gone."

Clermont simply nodded and exited the room, leaving Hugo to contemplate the bench in the square below.

The governess sat, turning her head to watch people passing on the pavement. She did not look as if she were about to burst into hysterics. Perhaps Clermont hadn't wronged her all that much, and he could solve this over the course of one conversation. He hoped so, for her sake.

Because if talk didn't work, he was going to have to make her life hell.

He hated having to do that.

⌘　⌘　⌘

It was hard for Miss Serena Barton to keep from fidgeting at the best of times; today, a chill wind had arisen in the afternoon, sending clouds scudding overhead and robbing the day of sunshine. The breeze sent autumn leaves rattling across the cobblestones. It sliced through her inadequate pelisse, and it was all she could do to refrain from wrapping her arms around herself. Still, she forced herself to sit, her spine straight. She wasn't going to freeze to death; she was just going to get very, very cold. Nothing that a cup of hot tea wouldn't fix when she returned to her sister's rooms that evening.

She glanced sidelong at the small cluster that had gathered on the gangway in front of the Duke of Clermont's home. In the lull of the late afternoon, a few servants had come by; they huddled in a little knot to gawk at her. No doubt they knew she'd talked to Clermont. She was counting on their gossip. Speculation would embarrass the man more than a simple recounting of the truth, and her only hope was to embarrass him a great deal. Speculation bred gossip; gossip gave rise to censure.

Three maids in ruffled aprons were whispering to one another when a man turned the corner onto the street. He scarcely seemed to notice them, but the group of women took one look at him and scattered to their respective houses, like hens fleeing a hawk overhead.

He didn't look like an aristocrat. He wore a brown suit, simply made, and a cravat, plainly tied. His linen was not the snowy-white that the wealthy insisted upon; his cuffs looked clean, but—as whites were wont to do upon washing—faded to a less respectable ivory. He stopped on the street just opposite her, and raised his head to meet her eyes.

For three months, Serena had wondered where she had gone wrong—what she could have done to avoid this fate. She'd retraced her steps a thousand times, searching for her error.

She'd been weak three months ago, when the duke had first found her—dropping her eyes for every man simply because he was bigger and stronger, holding her silence merely because it was improper to scream. Serena was done being weak.

She'd met the duke's gaze this morning, not flinching when she looked in his eyes and issued her threats. After that, she could do anything.

And this man wasn't a duke.

So she met his gaze. *I'm not afraid of you,* she thought. And if the clamminess of her palms declared otherwise, there was no need to tell him that.

But he was only a working man, if she read the middling-quality fabric of his jacket aright. Everything about him was middling. He wasn't particularly tall, nor was he short. He was neither skinny nor fat. The most that she could imagine anyone saying about him was that he was virulently moderate.

He looked *safe.* An utterly ridiculous thing to think, of course. Still, Serena held his eyes, smiled, and gave the fellow a polite, dismissive nod.

He crossed the street toward her.

He was as unremarkable as the shrubbery that edged the square. He had a nondescript face, so familiar that it might have belonged to anyone. He gave her a friendly, unassuming smile.

She did not respond in kind. She wasn't *nice,* she wasn't *easy,* and she was done being a target. She gave him a pointed look—a raise of her eyebrow that signified *don't you impinge on my time.*

A man as ordinary as this one should have flinched from her expression. But this one came right up to her bench and, without so much as asking her leave, sat next to her.

"Nice day," he commented.

His voice was like his face: not too high and not too deep. His accent was not the drawl of aristocratic syllables trained to lazy perfection, but a hint of something from the north.

"Is it?" It wasn't—not when she'd been sitting outside long enough to turn her nose red. Not when an unfamiliar man sat next to her and started a conversation.

She turned to frown at him.

He was watching her with a quizzical little smile. "I believe there is no good way to continue."

She sighed. "You've come for gossip, haven't you?"

"You could say that." He tensed, and then met her eyes. "It's Hugo Marshall, by the way." He tossed the introduction out, and then leaned back, as if waiting for her response.

Was he an important man? She remembered the servants scattering as he'd approached. Maybe he was a solicitor, who might carry tales. Or a butler, who enforced rules. He looked rather young to be a Mayfair butler, but whatever he was, he wasn't going away.

She would have preferred a woman to start the gossip—she found it easier to talk to women. But perhaps this fellow would do.

"Miss Serena Barton," she finally offered. "I suppose everyone wants to know why I'm here."

He shrugged, and gave her another one of those pleasant smiles. "I have no interest in everyone," he responded smoothly. "But I do wish you'd satisfy my individual curiosity. The accounts I have heard are quite garbled."

She had no intention of satisfying anything of his. She'd been cut deep by her own silence—cut to the point of shame. Now it was her turn to wield that knife.

The Duke of Clermont had told her to stay quiet. So she would.

"Accounts? What accounts?" she asked.

"I've heard you're Clermont's former mistress."

She raised a single eyebrow at that. Silence could cut both ways—for instance, when one failed to repudiate rumors that might cause damage. She wished Clermont much joy of her silence.

He tapped his fingers against the arm of the bench, holding her gaze. "I've heard you're a governess, and that Clermont promised you a position looking after his unborn child. When he reneged, you took to sitting outside here to shame him for not honoring his contracts."

That was so absurd that she couldn't stop herself from laughing.

He simply sighed. "No," he said. "Of course not."

If gossip was running to breach of contract, she needed a new strategy. But Serena simply smoothed her skirts over her knees. "My," she said. "Do keep talking. What else?"

He pushed his gloved hands together and looked down. "I've heard that Clermont forced himself on you." This last came out in a low growl.

Serena repressed a shiver. She didn't flinch—not even from the shadow that passed over her at that. "You believe all of this?"

"I believe none of it, not without proof. Tell me what really happened, Miss Barton, and perhaps I can help."

She'd told the duke everything that morning. He'd laughed and told her to take herself off and keep quiet. It was the second time he'd demanded her silence. So she'd promised to return it to him—silence, accusing silence. Weeks and weeks of it, sitting practically on his doorstep with everyone wondering. If the gossip threatened to reach his wife, he'd have to take responsibility.

She regarded Mr. Marshall now. For all his smiling affability, he was direct. He'd simply jumped into the matter and asked her right out. By the way he was watching her, he expected an answer.

On a second inspection, she decided he was not as ordinary as she'd supposed. His nose had been broken. It had also been set, but not very well, and so there was a bump in the middle of it. And while he wasn't fat, he was broader across the shoulders than any butler she'd seen.

But he was giving her an encouraging smile, and the warning prickle in her palms had faded to almost nothing. He was safe. Gossipy, perhaps, but safe.

"I'm sorry, Mr. Marshall," she said. "I really will not say."

"Oh?" He looked mildly puzzled. "You won't tell even me?"

"I don't dare." She gave him another smile. "I do apologize for piquing your curiosity, but I'll be unable to oblige it. Good day."

He took off his hat and rubbed his brown hair. "Is there some need for secrecy? I'll meet you in the dead of night, if that's what it takes to resolve the matter. I was hoping this would be simple."

Her smile froze. "No," she heard herself say distinctly. "These days, I only meet in sunlight. I don't mean to be so circumspect, but if I air my grievances to the public, it is possible that I could be charged with defamation of character. I must be careful." That was the right note to strike with the gossips—imply that she had the capacity to blacken the duke's name, without ever listing specifics.

But he didn't speculate. He leaned back, and the iron bench creaked. "You think Clermont would have you brought up for talking to me?"

"Oh, surely not Clermont himself. But his man… Who knows what he might do to keep the duke's secret?"

"His man," Mr. Marshall repeated, setting his hat next to him on the bench. "You won't talk to *me* because you're frightened of Clermont's man."

"Surely you've heard of him. They call him the Wolf of Clermont."

"They—what?" He pulled back.

"The Wolf of Clermont," she repeated. "The duke hires him to get things done, things that an ordinary man, fettered by a conscience, would not do."

He stared at her for a few moments. Then, ever so slowly, Mr. Marshall picked up his hat once more and turned it in his hands. "Ah," he said. "*That* Wolf of Clermont. You're acquainted with the fellow?"

"Oh, yes."

He made a polite sound of disbelief.

"From the gossip papers only," she explained. "I've never met him, of course. But he has the blackest of reputations. He was a pugilist before he took over the duke's affairs, and from what I've heard, he's handled His Grace's matters with all the aplomb that one could expect from a man who made his living prizefighting. They say that he's utterly ruthless. I can see him now: some squat, stocky man, all shoulders, no neck."

"All shoulders," he repeated softly. "No neck." His own hand rose, as if of its own accord, to touch his cravat. "Fascinating."

"But if you work near here, surely you must have seen him. Do I have the right of it?"

He gave her another one of his friendly smiles.

"Yes," he said softly. "You've described him precisely. If I were you, I'd not want to set myself opposite him. I'd think long and hard about that. And as you're not talking…" He picked up his hat and set it on his head. "I'll wish you a good day, Miss Barton. And much luck."

"Thank you."

"Don't thank me," he replied. "If you're in opposition to the Wolf of Clermont, luck won't do you any good. It will just make his chase interesting."

Chapter Two

ONCE AGAIN, SERENA'S SISTER had not left home all day.

Serena could tell because Frederica's cloak and gloves were still gathering dust on the small table in the entry. A bit of a stretch, to call this haphazardly walled-off section of hallway an "entry." The word brought to mind marble floors, crystal chandeliers, and liveried butlers who whisked hats and gloves away.

Here, there was only the rickety wood table and yellowing whitewash of an old house, once grand, now little better than tenement housing for women who had slipped into the depths of genteel poverty. The air was cold and musty.

Nonetheless, Serena removed her own cloak and gloves and set them next to Freddy's, and then peered into the adjoining chamber. She could scarcely make out the silhouettes of furniture in the unlit room. Oil and candles were dear, when one scraped by on fifteen pounds a year.

Freddy sat before the window, holding her sewing up so that the faint illumination from the street lamp shone on her work. Serena had been told she looked like her sister, but Freddy's skin was pale and her hair was orange, like their mother; Serena took her darker hair and skin from their father. If there was a resemblance, she'd never seen it.

"Good evening, dear," Freddy said absently, as she worked her needle through the cloth.

Serena came to stand behind her. "Good evening." She set her hands on her sister's shoulders, and gave her a light squeeze. "You've been working on this all day, haven't you? Your shoulders are so stiff."

"Just a few moments longer."

"You'll ruin your eyesight, sewing in this failing light."

"Mmm." Freddy made another precise stitch.

She was piecing together another quilt of interlocking rings. She didn't sell her work—that would have made her a laborer, and ladies, as Freddy so often explained, did *not* labor. Instead, Freddy gave her quilts away to charitable organizations. Almost half her extra income went to scraps and second-quality yarn for the deserving poor. More than half her time was spent knitting scarves and sewing blankets for babies. It didn't seem quite fair to Serena; without stirring from her rooms, her elder sister managed to make her feel both exhausted and inadequate.

Serena sighed.

"You don't have to do this, Freddy. Why do you force yourself to it?"

"Don't call me Freddy. You know I hate that name." Freddy laid down her work. "You don't have to do this, either. Serena, you know I love you, but this is not what we were born to do. Why must you bother Clermont? He hurt you once; why give him the chance to do so again?"

An image of a dark room tucked under the eaves darted into Serena's head. She could see Clermont ducking through the too-short doorway, could hear the sound of the door shutting behind him.

She shivered.

She wanted proof that she wasn't the sort to cower in the corner, no matter what had happened to her. She wanted to conquer that complex burden of shame and confusion and anger.

Serena set her hand over her still-flat belly. She had enough to contend with as it was.

"I want justice." The words were flat in her mouth, and yet sharp, so sharp. "I want to show that he can't win." Her fingers curled with want. "That he can't just—"

Freddy sniffed dismissively. "We've enough to survive on," she said as if money were a substitute for fair play. "Stay with me. I always said you should. But no; you had to run off governessing, when we were left with the sort of competence that could see us through our lives, if we economized."

"We were left fifteen pounds a year," Serena protested. Enough to avoid starvation; enough to have a roof over their heads. But every year, costs went up. It hadn't taken much forethought to see that in twenty years, expenses would outrun income.

"But," Freddy said, continuing with the lecture, "you had to want more. You've always wanted more. And see where it's left you? You can't eat justice."

No. But at least she wouldn't choke on it. Serena unclenched the fist she'd made at her side.

"By the by," Freddy said more casually, "where *has* it left you?"

"Without a position," Serena snapped. "With no hope of a character reference."

"All your fine plans," Freddy said, half scolding, half comforting, "and they've come to naught. Best not to dream, dear. If you don't, there's nothing that can be taken from you."

Pure cowardice, that. Freddy fretted when she had to cross the street to purchase milk. When she'd gone to meet Serena at the yard where the stagecoach had left her, she'd been white-lipped and trembling. She'd complained of pains in her chest all the way home. Freddy didn't handle change well, and nothing changed so often as the world outside her door.

There was a reason that Serena had signed away her portion of their father's bequest. Freddy could not have survived on her half, and she was incapable of making up the shortfall.

"All of your fine plans," Freddy repeated gently, "and here you are. With nothing. Less than nothing."

"No," she said thickly. "Not…not nothing."

"With nightmares and a babe on the way."

Serena kept her eyes wide open. Her hands trembled; she forced them to stillness, pushing them against her skirts until they grew steady. She imagined the spark of life growing inside her, gestating next to her bitter fury. Sometimes, she feared that all of that cold, trembling anger would eat her child alive. *Not after I win. Then I'll be safe, and I'll never be hurt again.*

"I told you already," she said. To her own ear, her voice seemed to come from very far away. "I don't have nightmares. I don't have time to be frightened of anything."

At her last position, the Wolvertons had obtained a microscope for their children's instruction in the natural world. They'd magnified everything. Sometimes, the memory that played itself through her dreams seemed like those enlarged images. The edges danced, overhung with the chromatic effect of a dark, shadowing halo. She felt as if she were looking at something very small, something very far away. So distant that it almost wasn't happening.

She had felt so helpless then, so utterly without recourse. She should have screamed. She should have bashed the duke over the head. She should have *fought*. In her memory of that night, her own silence mocked her most of all.

She hadn't screamed, and because she hadn't, she'd felt silent ever since.

Freddy simply sighed. "When you're ready to give up," she said, "I'll be here. But I don't know what you hope to accomplish, except to bring that horrid wolf-man down on both our heads."

This, at least, Serena could answer. "I have it on the best of authority," she said, "that he's a thickheaded fellow. All brawn and no brains. When it comes down to it, I'll simply outsmart him."

"Oh, dear." Freddy leaned over and tapped Serena's cheek. "When you fail, I'll be here to pick up the pieces. As usual."

⌘ ⌘ ⌘

HUGO HAD MORE THAN enough to do the following day. Nonetheless, thoughts of the governess followed him throughout his work. He sent out a man to discover what had *really* happened between his employer and Miss Serena Barton at Wolverton Hall. If she wouldn't tell him and Clermont wouldn't say, he'd have to find out on his own.

He spent the morning attempting to banish thoughts of her—of that chestnut hair, bound into a loose knot, waiting to become unpinned. Her eyes were gray and still, like water too long undisturbed. Her hands had been quiet—unmoving.

By the afternoon, he gave up the cause of work as hopeless and wandered to the window. He'd caught glimpses of her sitting on her bench all morning. Now, she sat still as a statue, scarcely moving, scarcely *breathing*, and yet somehow completely alive.

She wasn't what he would have called pretty. Handsome, yes. And there was something about her eyes… He shook his head; her appearance was hardly relevant.

He'd been testing her yesterday, mentioning rape. It was…horrifyingly possible. He wasn't sure what he would have done if she'd confirmed his fears. He'd done a great many things on Clermont's behalf, but he'd never hurt a woman. Even his wounded conscience had its limits.

But she'd not even flinched when he'd said the word. She hadn't reacted to anything at all.

And therein lay his second problem. When he'd introduced himself, he'd assumed that she would recognize his name. But she had apparently gleaned his reputation entirely through gossip columns, and they only ever referred to him as the Wolf of Clermont. There was no reason anyone who had just arrived in London *would* know his name.

He should have corrected her misapprehension.

He hadn't, and he wasn't sure why. Just an instinct. For all the duke's blasé reassurances, he suspected that whatever was at the heart of this quarrel was a scandal—and one that could undo all of Hugo's fine work. He couldn't fix the problem if he didn't know what he was facing, and if she worked herself up into a fear of him, he might never learn the truth—not until he saw it on the front page of a newspaper.

Still, he didn't like lying. Not even by implication.

"Whatever you are up to, Miss Barton," he whispered, "you will not cost me my five hundred pounds. I have worked too hard for it."

Fifty yards on the other side of the pane of glass, she swung her head, startling him with the sudden movement. He stepped back—but she was only watching a bird that had landed on the ground in front of her.

With a sigh, Hugo pushed the rest of his papers aside. No sense wasting any more time wondering, when he could be finding out.

He exited the house via the servants' door, tromped back through the mews, and then back 'round to the street. Miss Barton was still sitting there when he crossed into the square. She gave him a smile, this one a little warmer than the one he'd received yesterday.

There was something about her that drew his eye.

"Mr. Marshall," she said. "I did say you wouldn't be successful in your quest for gossip, did I not?"

"You wound me." He didn't smile, and her own expression fluttered uncertainly. "You assume that I only have interest in gossip, when in fact, I might just be searching out your company for the sheer pleasure of it."

She thought this over, tilting her head to one side. Then: "I have now considered that possibility. I reject it. Come, Mr. Marshall. Tell me you didn't come out here hoping for some sordid story."

"So you admit the story is sordid."

She wagged her finger at him. "I am guessing as to your own thoughts. There's no need to prevaricate. I know what people are saying about me. Secretly, you're judging me, and you've already found me wanting. You're all saying that I'm no better than I should be."

Hugo shrugged. "I've never understood that saying—no better than you should be. Why would anyone *want* to be better than required? I only behave when it counts; I wouldn't begrudge you similar conduct."

She stared at him a moment.

He was misleading her enough as it is. He had no intention of outright lying to her. "You don't believe me," he said. "I can't help it—it's my face. It makes everyone think that I'm quite friendly, when anyone who knows better will warn you off. I'm entirely ruthless. Quite without morals."

The smile she gave him was patronizing. "Is that so? Well. I'm sure you're a very, very bad man. I'm so scared."

Hugo looked upward. "Drat."

"Drat?" She hid a smile. "Surely a man as awful as you could conjure up a 'damn' in mixed company."

"I don't swear," he explained. "Not in any company."

"I see. You *are* bad."

He glanced at the sky in exasperation. "I am aware that this fact in isolation hardly proves my point. Which is this: If you wish to speak to me in confidence, if you wish to tell your tale without fear of judgment, I'm your man. Nobody would dare to gossip with me."

She stared at him. "You're very convincing," she said, in a tone that implied she believed anything but. "But you are…what, an accountant? Someone who keeps the household books?"

He nearly choked. "You could say that," he finally said. "I suppose I make sure the books balance at the end of the day."

She gave him a patronizing nod of the head. "All that ruthlessness, and only the books to balance. Poor Mr. Marshall." She smiled at him. "I consider myself a good judge of character. And you, sir, are safe."

Safe.

It had been so long since someone *hadn't* taken him seriously that he'd forgotten what it was like. But here she was, dismissing him.

He sat gingerly on the edge of her bench.

"Maybe I am safe," he said. "I don't swear. I don't drink spirits, either." He took a deep breath. "You're sitting here for a reason, though, Miss Barton, and I doubt it's for your health. Is it so wrong of me to want to help?"

All the latent humor bled from her face. "Help," she repeated blankly. "You want to *help*."

"This is no triviality before you. A lady does not risk the wrath of a duke without reason. I don't want to see you hurt."

"Why not?" she asked. "If you're so ruthless."

He smiled in spite of himself. "*Ruthless* doesn't mean that I survey the available options and gleefully choose the cruelest one. It means that I solve problems, whatever the cost. I'm *good* at that."

"And so out of the goodness of your heart, you're offering—"

"No," he said, leaning in. "You misunderstand. There's no goodness in my heart—that's what I keep trying to explain to you. You are a problem. It distracts me from my work to think of you here. To wonder…"

She sucked in her breath and pulled away from him slightly. Her eyes seemed round and very gray. She scarcely moved. The air around them seemed suddenly charged. He couldn't look away from her, and he could almost hear his words echoed back at him.

It distracts me to think of you.

It was almost nothing, that faint sense of attraction he felt. It was no more than the scarcely-heard hum of an insect. Insignificant enough that he waved it away. But she had just noticed, and that small hint of interest, mild though it had been, had washed the smile from her face.

"Go away," she said, her voice flat.

No, she wasn't here because of an employment dispute. Clermont had a great deal to answer for.

Hugo reached down and plucked a spare twig from the ground and set it on the bench between them. "This," he said, "is a wall, and I will not cross it."

Her eyes fixed on that piece of wood, a few scant inches in length.

"I don't believe in hurting women," he said.

She did not respond.

"I do a great many things, and I'm not proud of many of them. But I don't swear. I don't drink. And I don't hurt women. I don't do any of those things because my father did every one." He held her eyes as he spoke. "Now I've told you something that nobody else in London knows. Surely you can return the favor. What is it you want?"

She shook her head slowly. "No, Mr. Marshall. I will not be browbeaten, however nicely you do it. I am done with things happening to me. From here on out, *I* am going to happen to things."

She raised her head as she spoke. And that annoying hum—that gnat-like buzz of attraction that he had so easily brushed away—seemed to swell around him like a growing murmur of wind.

Her features seemed so crisp, outlined against the cool air. She had not a hair out of place. Still, she made him think of a bear, strong and certain, claiming her territory at the top of a mountain.

Here, he thought, *finally, was a match for him.*

There was no point being fanciful. What use had he with a bear? Still… Surely he could appreciate one when he saw it.

"Brave words," he said softly. "That's what it means to be ruthless. After all, I happen to other people on a regular basis."

She glanced pointedly at the twig between them.

Hugo made no move toward her. "I don't suppose you know why they call him the Wolf of Clermont."

"His ruthlessness."

"But the specifics. You know how he came to work with Clermont?"

She shook her head.

He steepled his fingers and looked away from her. "Clermont would never have hired a pugilist as his man of business. But he always did like prizefights. And drinking; all dukes love to drink. He became inebriated one day after a fight, and spilled all his troubles to the champion."

"Dukes surely have a great many troubles." She rolled her eyes.

"It was the usual litany: old title, nothing but bills to show for it, and a less than sterling reputation to boot. The Wolf wagered him one hundred pounds that in six months, he could rearrange everything so that he'd have no more bill collectors hammering on his doors."

She was watching him. "How do you know this?"

He waved his hand. "Everyone knows this—all the servants around here, in any event."

She nodded. "Go on. If this Wolf is to be my nemesis, I need to know everything about him."

"Clermont was not without resources. His estates brought in a pittance—with a few months' grace, and the benevolence of a few lenders, all might have been brought around. But the duke didn't have a few months. And so the Wolf focused on the duke's most prominent creditor. Everyone has secrets, and that creditor's secret was that his money had been made in the slave trade years after it had been banned. The Wolf made sure every sordid detail went to the papers. The family was shunned. And do you know what the Wolf did then?"

She shook her head.

He looked her in the eyes. "He paid the debt," he said. "Publicly. Without once having to voice a threat, the Wolf made Clermont untouchable. Insist on payment, the gossips said, and he'd ruin you. Startling, the number of people who are willing to agree to easier terms of payment when their own future is on the line."

"Why are you telling me this?"

"Miss Barton," he said quietly, "with whom do you think you are speaking?"

She sucked in air. But her expression did not change one iota at that confession.

"You see how it is," Hugo said. "I *am* going to get rid of you. But ruining someone is a messy, complicated business. It is much less work to help you than to break you. Let me help."

She had not taken her eyes off him during that speech.

"What do you want?" he asked.

"I want him to pay." Her chin lifted. She folded her hands—a dainty motion—but there was nothing dainty in the determined way her fingers tangled together.

"Money?"

"Recognition." Her jaw squared. "He wants me to stay silent. Well, I want him to speak out. To feel one-tenth of the censure that I have."

There was no chance of that. No wonder Clermont had passed this woman's demands on to Hugo. Any form of recognition would destroy the duke's chances at reconciling with his duchess. With so much at stake, including Hugo's own five hundred pounds...

"He'll never do that," he said. "I like you, Miss Barton. I don't wish to have you on my conscience."

She picked up the twig he'd laid across the bench and held it out to him. "Do your worst," she said. "That *is* what you're known for, is it not?"

He stared at the twig in her hand for a few moments before taking it from her and laying it back across the bench. "I will," he said. "If I have to. I'd prefer not to."

⌘ ⌘ ⌘

THE INK FROM THE evening paper had stained Serena's gloves black, but still she stood on the street corner, trying to make out the advertisements on the back page without straining her eyes.

Rents for properties with small acreage were close to fifteen pounds per annum, and with expenses calculated at almost twice that, plus sustenance and the cost of someone to stay with her...

Once, she'd dreamed of what she'd do with the money she carefully set aside from the wages she earned as a governess. She'd planned to lease a small farm, to grow lavender, when she had saved enough. From there, her wistful hopes had built a thousand possibilities. Freddy had pooh-poohed her ambitions, and perhaps she had the right of it. Purchasing a paper now, when her dreams had never been so far away, was the height of foolishness. It served only to underscore how much she had lost—how far removed her girlish dreams were from reality.

Serena had forty pounds saved from three years of wages. She had enough for the present, but not so much that she could afford to dwell on the past. But she could not get free of her situation by escaping into an elaborate day-dream. Reality waited for her: She was pregnant, and she had no income.

Serena folded the paper in quarters, hiding away the list of properties for lease and looked up into the darkening night.

She made herself repeat those damning words. She was pregnant. She had no income. And she had just suffered a blow—a terrible blow.

Mr. Marshall had seemed so *safe,* so ordinary. She had not felt so comfortable around a man in months. When he'd picked up that twig and set it between them, some foolish part of her had really believed it was a wall, and that she might breathe easily.

He'd made her dream of a might-have-been: an afternoon spent with a man who made her smile, who didn't look at her as if she were some ruined thing. She'd dreamed of a world where any future could be open, if only she could find the right key. She'd wanted attraction. Affection. Security.

Love.

Foolish to leap from a conversation in a square to love. But if one man might smile and converse with her, a second could as well.

As she'd sat on that bench, her might-have-beens had glowed with sunlight.

But Mr. Marshall was no smiling, friendly fellow. He was the Wolf of Clermont, a man known for his mercilessness. With a few sparse sentences he'd smashed all her hopeful might have beens into a single *wasn't.*

Her future stretched like a dark road before her: all hope in eclipse.

He'd fooled her. *I do not curse. I do not drink spirits. And I don't hurt women. I don't do any of those things because my father did every one.*

Serena crumpled the paper.

He was good—very good. And she was the damned fool who had teetered on the brink of trusting him. But he'd offered to help not because he took an interest in her affairs, or because he cared about her welfare. It was just because it was simpler to buy her off than ruin her.

Black clouds loomed on her horizon.

Serena set her hand on her stomach. Despair couldn't be good for the baby. When she let it settle around her, it seemed to fill her belly with a bitter, starving impossibility. She could scarcely digest it; how could a life so fragile and tiny manage what she could not?

No. Her baby would have no nightmares, no doubts, no fears.

When one climbed trees, it was a fool's game to look down. If one did, one risked vertigo. So Serena looked up now, past the oncoming gloom of the night. She focused on the warm orange glow of the lamp and the dimmer light of the stars beyond. She looked up and refused to think of falling.

Chapter Three

PERHAPS HE WAS GROWING SOFT, but Hugo started with the most simple of expedients. He tried to rid himself of Miss Barton by taking her seat. It cost him all of six shillings to hire four pensioners to sit on her spot on the bench. He watched her arrive early the next morning. She drew up when she saw that the bench was occupied, and then set her hand in the small of her back. Just that little note of complaint. Then she smiled, shook her head, and walked idly around the square, as if she'd planned to perambulate in any event. She glanced at the old men as she walked. She made another slow circuit, and then another. After half an hour, she seemed to realize they weren't leaving.

Her chin lifted. She looked over at Clermont's house as if she could see Hugo inside. As if she were *daring* him to do worse. She stood all day, her head held high, and if she occasionally rubbed her hips when she thought nobody was looking, or shifted from foot to foot in discomfort, it only served to make Hugo feel worse about what he was doing.

On the second day, she arrived an hour earlier, while the streetlamps were still lit. She strode sedately toward the bench—and stopped abruptly.

Hugo had anticipated her early arrival, of course, and he'd offered the pensioners seven shillings for that extra hour. Once again, she stayed standing on her feet for nine straight hours—disappearing only, he supposed, to use the necessary. Once again, he found himself admiring her obstinacy.

On the third day, it rained. The rain fell in great gusting torrents, and the pensioners couldn't be had. Still, Hugo managed to round up a few laborers dressed in mackintosh—and scarcely in time. They had just settled in when Miss Barton arrived. She was swathed in a cloak of dark wool, one that covered her gown. He couldn't see her hair, couldn't see her hands.

After an hour, her umbrella was so sodden that it no longer repelled water; she abandoned it next to a tree. But she didn't let the wet stop her. She scarcely looked at the bench. Instead, she stood next to a tree, her lips set in grim determination.

He watched her throughout the morning. Midday, he stopped work for a bowl of soup. She was still there; he ate, standing at the window, watching as she pulled her arms around herself and rubbed briskly, trying to stay warm.

She was going to catch her death. The wind was blowing leaves about; it had to be bitter cold. Noon turned to one o'clock, and then two. She hadn't left when the clock in the hall chimed three, even though her cloak had turned dark with rain. She huddled in on herself more and more.

Anyone else would have gone home at the first sign of inclement weather. He wasn't sure if he should applaud her tenacity or rage at how impossible she'd made the situation. Down in the square, she swiped a hand over her face, brushing away rainwater.

This was something that Hugo was going to have to fix, if for no other reason than that he didn't want her life on his head.

⌘　⌘　⌘

BEFORE SERENA'S CLOAK soaked through, it hadn't been so bad. She'd been damp and rather cold. But having to stand had been a blessing in disguise; she'd been able to warm herself by walking.

By the time the clock struck three, though, she could scarcely feel her feet. Her hands were frozen inside her gloves.

Go home. It's only one afternoon.

It wasn't loud, that impulse. Just insidious. She'd heard it too often. *Keep quiet now, and you'll be taken care of. Don't scream tonight; it will stop soon enough.* But that voice was a lie. Those who did nothing lost. There was nothing so cold as regret.

If she walked away now, Mr. Marshall would know that he *could* drive her away. It would just spur him on to greater efforts.

And so she chafed her hands together and paced.

Nobody was out unless he had to be. And so that was why, when a figure came around the corner, she turned to look—and then froze. It was Mr. Marshall—the Wolf of Clermont, she reminded herself—looking very grim. He had a bundle under his arm. He walked, head down. When he came abreast of her, he glanced down the street and crossed quickly.

He walked right past her without saying a word, and instead marched up to the men sitting on the bench. She had struggled to see the Wolf of Clermont in him when he'd confessed his identity three days past, but in that instant, she saw it. His ordinariness was an illusion, a cloak of normalcy that he donned for politeness's sake. Now, he projected a quiet menace—one so palpable that she stepped back, raising her hand to her throat, even though his ire wasn't directed at her. He fixed the men on the bench with a look.

"Well?" he asked. "Get out of here."

"But—" said one.

"You heard what I said. It's over. I have no more need of you. Get out of here." He gave his head a little jerk.

The men exchanged glances, and then, one by one, they stood and filed out of the square. Serena raised her hands to her lips and blew on them, trying to warm them through her sodden gloves. But Mr. Marshall didn't look at her. He unfolded his bundle. It was, oddly enough, a load of towels wrapped around an umbrella. He laid the towels out on the bench, drying the seat. Then he popped open the umbrella and motioned her over.

"Sit," he said. His features were stone.

She was too bedraggled—and too cold—to object to being ordered about. She came over and sat. He hooked the umbrella to the back of the seat, fastening it in place with a bit of rope so that it shielded her half of the bench from rain. Then he unrolled a second towel and took out a metal flask, an irregular package wrapped in wax paper, and, inexplicably, a teacup. He handed her the cup. "Hold this."

She tried to take it in her hands, but her fingers were too cold to grasp properly and it slipped away.

He caught it midair and glared at her, as if it were her fault her hands could not grip. Without saying a word, he took hold of her wrist and, before she could protest, he had slipped a finger beneath her glove.

She jerked spasmodically away; his grip tightened in reaction. He raised his head, met her eyes, and became very still.

She could count his breaths. She could feel her pulse thrumming in her wrist, encased in his fingers.

Slowly, he let go.

"My apologies," he said. "I was not thinking. I was going to take off your gloves and rub some sensation into your fingers. Can you do it on your own?"

She fumbled with her own glove, but the material clung to her skin and she could scarcely feel what she was doing.

"Will you let me?" he asked.

Serena met his eyes. He'd dropped his air of menace, and—even knowing full well how wrong the notion was—that same sense returned to her. *Safe. Safe. This man is safe.*

Ridiculous.

Nonetheless, Serena held out her hands to him.

He took off one glove and then the other, touching her only long enough to work the fabric down her fingers.

The air was cold against her bare skin, but the sensation lasted only a few seconds. He set her gloves aside, wrapped her hands in a towel and rubbed them vigorously.

The touch should have felt intimate and invasive. His hands engulfed hers. And he'd practically disrobed her—well, maybe dis*gloved* her. But he was so matter-of-fact about it that his touch felt…normal.

Safe, the back of her mind whispered.

He left her hands wrapped in the towel, like some oversized muff, and then picked up the metal flask. It looked like the sort of container in which gentlemen stored gin—flat and thin. But he unscrewed the cap and a curl of steam escaped.

Serena sighed in longing. He poured the contents—a glorious golden-brown—into the teacup, and then held it out to her. "I don't know how you take your tea," he said, "and I had no way to bring the cream and sugar out here. I added both. I can only hope the result is palatable."

She maneuvered a hand out of the towel and took the cup. Her hand was still shaking; he watched her with narrowed eyes. But the cup was warm—so warm that it seared her skin. And the tea… Oh, it was lovely. Strong and sweet, with a generous dollop of creamy milk.

The first sip seemed to thaw the ice in her fingers.

"Why are you doing this?"

"I told you," he said. "I don't hurt women."

"You're hardly responsible for my presence here. I'm here by dint of my own willful stubbornness." She took another gulp of tea.

"Semantics," he returned. "You're here. Who is to blame, if I am not?"

"The Duke of Clermont comes to mind. You're his charge, not the other way around."

Mr. Marshall snorted. "Is that what you think?"

She took another swallow of tea rather than answer the question. "This is the best tea I have ever had," she said. "Thank you."

"Don't thank me."

Her gaze locked with his, and she found herself unable to look away. His eyes were brown—light, like the color of sunlight filtered through autumn leaves. He was so focused on her, the entire world seemed to melt away—the dark clouds overhead, the puddles underfoot. There was nothing but him.

It had been more than three months since she'd felt even the mildest hints of sexual attraction. She'd thought it had been burned from her for good, stolen by fear and the cold, clutching hands of dark memory. Apparently not. Her better sense could be swayed by two swallows of tea and an umbrella.

Safe. He is safe.

But no matter that he'd brought her shelter and warmth, there was nothing safe about him.

Mr. Marshall smiled at her—not the easy smile of a mild acquaintance, but a smile with a sharp edge. Still, he stayed on his half of the bench. Rain collected on the brim of his hat and dripped over the edges, but it did not make him look in the least disheveled.

"You could have sent another servant out with an umbrella. You didn't have to come yourself."

"I assumed it would unsettle you more if I fed you in person," he answered.

"Feed me? You haven't—"

"Ah. Thank you for the reminder." He unfolded a package wrapped in waxed paper, revealing some squashed sandwiches filled with a strange green and pink mixture.

"I shouldn't."

He snorted. "You shouldn't be standing in a square in the rain. Your hands shouldn't be so cold that you can't properly wrap them around a teacup. I hate to think what you are doing to your lungs, breathing this cold, wet air for hours on end. You're risking your health. In what possible world can you do all those things and yet not have a sandwich?" He held out the waxed paper to her. "Eat."

"You're trying to browbeat me again." Still, she took his offering and nibbled at the edge. She wasn't sure what was in it—some kind of smoked ham, maybe. Diced cucumber was easier to recognize. It was delicious, although she suspected that had more to do with her hunger and the cold than the actual sandwich.

He refilled her teacup.

She swallowed. "You're too kind."

"No, I'm not," he contradicted. "I'm deliberately confusing you out of a desire to assuage my own meager excuse for a conscience. To add to my sins, in defiance of all society's rules, I wish to become better acquainted with you. Don't imagine there's anything akin to kindness behind my selfish behavior."

The umbrella had slowly tilted to one side behind them, and it had begun to drip on the towel—plop, plop, plop, slow and steady.

"Society's rules?" she said. "When a gentleman condescends to a ruined woman, it's called kindness. No matter what his motives might be."

He straightened the umbrella. "I'm no gentleman."

She stared at him—at his well-made coat and the half-sandwich still wrapped in waxed paper, set off to his side. "You work for a duke."

"You're a lady who had to stoop to governessing. I make a good game of it, but my father was a coal miner in Yorkshire. I'm the fourteenth of sixteen children. I made my living with my fists for a handful of years."

"You sound as if you're from the north." But not quite. He spoke in a clipped rhythm that made her think of London—fast and frenetic. There was a hint of a burr there, a roll to his words. But it had softened and smoothed out. "But how does a miner become a…a…"

He smiled. "I don't know what I am, either."

"Nonetheless. You're in charge of a duke's finances. I would have thought one required a certain amount of education in order to do that."

"Charity school," he said. "Also, I was small for my age, and so my mother convinced my father I was too young to go into the mines. She did that for years. He never could keep track of all his children. So when my younger brothers passed away, he became confused as to my age. I got rather a better education than might otherwise have been usual."

He was looking off into the distance as he spoke. But for all that his words seemed matter-of-fact, there was something about what he'd said— the thought of his mother lying to his father for the sake of his education, and his father not *noticing*—that sent a chill down her spine.

"I was fourteen when they first expected me to go into the mines." He turned back to her. "Old, really. Old enough to know better. I had watched the mines age men before their time. A year in the mines was worth ten years out. It was death working there—the only question was whether that death came slow or came on quick." He handed her another sandwich. "I was a miner for three days. I couldn't stand feeling that I was enclosed on all sides. So I ran away from home."

"What did you do instead?"

"Any work I could get my hands on." He looked away. She had no idea what kind of work a fourteen-year-old child would do, but she suspected that this man, dressed in clean and sober clothing, might not want to admit to being a common laborer. "But I knew what I wanted. I've always known what I wanted, ever since I left."

"You wanted to be a duke's right-hand man?" she asked dubiously.

"This?" He looked down, as if surprised to see himself, and then shook his head. "No. I've never aspired to serve anyone. But it's as good a way as any to meet those involved in business. And the money… By the time I'm forty, I'm going to have my own empire. I intend to be the richest coal miner's son in all of England. This is just the first step in getting there." He grinned at her. "Did I shock you? I know I'm supposed to declare my undying devotion to the man I serve."

"I have no fondness for that particular man," Serena said. "As you may recall."

He was smiling at her. He shouldn't be doing that. He shouldn't be doing any of this. Her hands tingled where his had so recently touched her. Her breath caught with the normalcy of this.

Well. Perhaps *normalcy* was not the right word. There was nothing ordinary about being seated next to her enemy in a driving rainstorm, drinking tea and chatting about life in the mines.

But there was his smile. She'd thought of the Wolf of Clermont as the duke's tool, his *thing*. Yet Mr. Marshall was sitting in the rain feeding her sandwiches. Maybe this was some twisted, diabolical strategy on his part. It seemed unlikely. It would have made more sense to keep her cold and hungry.

Her heart beat hard, half fear, half excitement. This was the man who, if the gossip papers had it right, had brought Clermont's estates back from the verge of imminent doom. The duke relied on him for everything. Without him, Clermont was nothing.

She could steal him away.

That thought—that she might rob the duke of someone so valuable—put her in sympathy with Mr. Marshall. He didn't want to be her enemy. Well, he didn't have to be.

Serena took a deep breath.

"I was never good at devotion myself," she admitted. "When I was a governess, I saved money because I wanted my own farm. Not a large one," she added, as he cocked his head in puzzlement. "I wanted to grow lavender and lilac. I taught myself how to extract the essence of the lavender plant. I was going to make fine-milled soaps and package them in dainty boxes and sell them at a tremendous profit to ladies who did not know any better."

His eyebrow twitched upward. "Ambitious," he remarked.

"Why do it, then?" she asked him. "Why drive me away, if not out of loyalty to the duke?"

He hesitated a beat before answering. "As it is," he finally said, "I *have* granted my unswerving devotion to someone."

He was looking at her with a steadfast, earnest look. Her heart fluttered. He couldn't mean *her*. It was too soon—they scarcely knew one another. And yet the way he was looking at her...

"Oh?" she heard herself answer.

He gave her a wicked smile and leaned an inch closer. She felt as if she were the only person in the world—as if the rain and cold had disappeared in the blaze of his eyes.

"I am devoted to me," he said. "My fortune rises and falls with the duke's. I do not *wish* to see your life in ruins, but I will not give up my chance to be someone just for you."

Serena swallowed.

"Your tea is getting cold." He gestured.

She took a sip. The liquid had cooled. With the edge off her appetite, she became aware that the tea was not perfect. She could taste a faintly metallic tang, and it had grown tepid and slightly bitter.

But there was nothing tepid about the attraction between them. She *could* steal him, if only she knew how.

He sat back, crossing his arms, and that moment of warmth passed. "Miss Barton," he said, slowly and distinctly, "do not make this any worse for yourself than it must be. I'll give you fifty pounds, and we'll manufacture a reference for you so that you may obtain another position."

She met his eyes. "That's all you want with me—to convince me to leave?"

"No." He spoke calmly. "But what I want with you is neither here nor there. I *need* you to go away, and so go away you shall."

"Not for fifty pounds and a reference," Serena answered just as calmly. "How could you think a reference would paper over what happened to me? I want justice, Mr. Marshall. Not a *reference*."

He leaned toward her. "Did he force you?" There was something of a snarl in his voice.

Her breath caught. That night—that horrible night—recreated itself in her mind, filling her with shame and guilt and regret. She was temporarily robbed of speech, consumed by the unending silence.

She forced herself to swallow that bitter swirl of emotion. She raised her chin and looked him in the eyes.

"No." Her voice broke on the word, but she did not look down. "He did not force me."

I let him do it.

There may have been a touch of pity in his eyes, a hint of gentleness as he took the teacup from her hands. But there was not the slightest trace of charity in his voice when he spoke. "Then it's fifty pounds and a reference," he said. "And not one iota of revenge."

Chapter Four

THE MESSENGER RETURNED FROM Wolverton Hall the day after the rain. Hugo stood at the window of his office, looking over the square below.

It was dry today, and the pensioners were back on the solitary bench. If he read a rebellious cast into her stance… What did it matter? It would change nothing.

He didn't take his eyes from her, but he was still aware of the messenger standing behind him.

"So," he finally said. "What happened?"

He'd sent Charles Gordon to find things out. The man was thin and weedy, and more than a little scared of Hugo. From the corner of his eye, Hugo saw the other man swallow, and stare straight in front of him.

"She didn't leave," Gordon said, licking his lips. "She was turned off for immoral behavior."

"Lying? Thievery?" Hugo's voice was even—all too even. He knew what was coming; she'd told him herself.

"The general gist of the gossip is that she took a man to her bed. In the house, if you'll believe it."

"She was caught in the act?"

"Someone saw him leaving her rooms."

"Ah." Hugo touched his fingertips together. "When you say, someone saw him…was the man in question identified?"

"No. The second housemaid saw a darkened figure leaving the female servants' quarters."

"Why did suspicion fall upon her, then? Had she a beau? A flirtation of some kind with a man?"

He asked the questions, but his mind was already racing far ahead. She'd admitted the duke hadn't forced her. Had he made her promises? Seduced her?

"No," Gordon said. "But when the matter was raised, they checked. There was blood on her sheets, and it wasn't her time."

A little shock went through him at all that implied. In the square below, Miss Barton raised her chin. He couldn't make out her features, but he could remember her gray eyes snapping at him as she spoke.

How could you imagine that fifty pounds and a reference would paper over what happened to me? she'd asked.

She'd been a virgin. That meant that Clermont had acted badly—even worse than Hugo had supposed. She'd claimed she hadn't been forced. But there were degrees of force, and all the ones that suggested themselves here made Hugo the villain in this particular drama.

He resented that Clermont had foisted that role upon him.

"If you need to rid yourself of her," Gordon said, "a few words about this in the right ears, and she'll be driven off in no time at all."

She would be. There had been a similar case last year—a lady's maid dismissed for indecent conduct. He'd seen the whole thing from his window. The other servants had crowded around her in the square when she left with her single valise. They'd jostled her. They'd called her names, ones he'd heard from even this distance, with a pane of glass and fifty feet between them. They'd called her *whore* and *slut,* and those had hardly been the worst of the epithets hurled. He'd been halfway down the stairs to put an end to the riot when someone had thrown a rock.

Somehow, the sight of her blood had been as effective at dispersing the crowd as a legion of constables wielding billyclubs.

Hugo had few pretensions about his own morals. He'd done a number of things that didn't skirt the boundaries of ethical conduct so much as trample through them. But he didn't like thinking of Miss Barton at the center of such a crowd. It wasn't a faceless throng that he saw around her when he envisioned that, but his own father looming, broom in hand.

You'll never bloody amount to anything, boy, so get back out there—

"Well?" Gordon asked. "Am I to spread the story?"

"No."

"That seems…awfully kind," Gordon said dubiously.

"Nothing of the sort."

It was simple self-preservation. If someone threw a rock at Miss Barton, Hugo was liable to kill him in cold blood. He would never achieve any of his ambitions if he hanged for murder.

Besides, the whole point was to keep Clermont's name out of the business. If she were labeled a slut, it would take the gossips a few short hours to decide who she'd been playing the slut *with.*

There were better ways to drive her away. The pressure he'd applied so far was mere child's play.

He didn't want to do it. He liked her. He admired her. There was something about her that wouldn't leave him alone. It ran entirely against his grain to crush the dreams and ambitions of a woman like her.

All the more reason she had to go. Every time he talked to her, he became more entangled.

It was time to truly flex his muscle. Gordon was not the only man he'd sent out to make inquiries. He waved the other man back a few steps, turned from the window, and opened the file he'd made on Miss Barton.

For the moment, Miss Barton lived with her sister, Miss Frederica Barton, in an attic room in Cheapside. The elder Miss Barton subsisted on the income from an annuity deposited at Daughtry's Bank.

"No," he repeated, more to convince himself than anything. "It's time to end the matter."

She was lovely and brave and all too stubborn. In some other world, he would have pursued a woman like her until he won her for his own. He would have stoked the attraction between them until it grew to a crackling heat. But he had no patience for wistful imaginings. It wasn't companionship that he hungered for deep down.

It might be fine indeed to take her for his own. But it wasn't the want of a woman that stole his sleep. He woke up remembering his father standing over him broom in hand, the smell of liquor on his breath.

You'll never amount to anything. Your filthy life isn't worth the bloody rags you're wearing.

No. There was an abyss of need inside him, but no woman could fill it. No matter how resolutely this one looked into his eyes.

Hugo reached for his inkwell and dipped his pen. Gordon watched as he scrawled something on the paper, sealed it, added the direction, and then handed it over.

"Deliver this," he said.

⌘　⌘　⌘

It had been a long day for Serena, made longer by the simple fact that nothing had happened. She'd told Mr. Marshall to do his worst. But he'd simply filled the bench with other people and left her alone.

After their tête-à-tête on the bench, she'd expected something. *Anything* other than nothing.

She opened the door to her sister's apartment with a sigh.

"Freddy?" she called.

Freddy didn't answer. The room was too silent. There was no clicking of knitting needles, no rustling of fabric. But her sister's things were still hanging in the entryway, and besides, she wouldn't have gone out. Not this close to dusk. Serena frowned and walked into the other room.

Freddy sat in her chair, her arms wrapped tightly around herself. She rocked back and forth ever so slightly, her whole body trembling. On the floor, lying in a forlorn heap, was a half-finished baby's blanket.

"Freddy, whatever is the matter?"

"Read it," Freddy said. Her voice shook. She jerked her chin at the table before her. "Read it."

There was a letter on the table. Serena didn't know what to think. She snatched it up and skimmed it quickly. It was from Freddy's landlord. "It has come to my attention…" she muttered, reading aloud at first. But her breath caught on the next sentence. She couldn't even speak those words. By the time she got to the end, she was breathless with rage.

She'd thought that the Wolf of Clermont had left her alone today. Ha. She looked at her sister, her arms wrapped about herself. It was one thing to annoy Serena herself. It was quite another to do harm to Freddy.

Freddy wasn't involved in this dispute. She'd never done anything—not since the dreadful night when she'd been in the carriage with their mother when it was robbed. She'd been sitting right next to her when the highwayman had taken his shot.

Freddy had never spoken of the event—but she'd scarcely been able to leave the house after. Serena had thought her distress would fade, but as the years went by, her sister had only come to fear the world outside her door more and more. Striking at her, and in this despicable way…

Mr. Marshall had a great deal to answer for.

Serena set the letter on the table.

"I have had quite enough," she said, her voice shaking with rage. "I will not—*will not*—let this happen to you, Freddy. I promise."

⌘   ⌘   ⌘

THE DOOR AT CLERMONT HOUSE was hard, but Serena pounded on it with all the force she could muster.

It was the third time that she'd knocked, and she wasn't expecting an answer. Still, she wasn't leaving until she obtained one. After what she'd come home to last night…

She raised her hand once more, and the door swung open. A gray-haired man peered down at her. Serena drew herself up to the full extent of her height—which unfortunately, didn't even bring her to the other man's shoulder.

"I demand to speak to Mr. Marshall," she said, with as much dignity as she could muster. "I demand to speak to him now."

The footman looked down his nose at her. "He is unavailable at the moment."

"Make him available. If he doesn't speak to me—"

"I have been instructed to give you this." The footman held out one hand; a crisp piece of white paper was folded in his fingers.

Slowly, she reached out and took it. It had been folded in a square; a firm hand had written "Miss Barton" across the front.

"And this," the footman said.

She looked up. The man held a pencil. It looked out of place in his white-gloved hands—too mundane to exist in such close proximity to a duke's livery. She took that, too, and was unfolding the missive when the door shut, firmly and irrevocably, behind her. Serena took the letter across the street and broke the seal.

Miss Serena Barton, she read. *It will behoove you to calm yourself. Convincing Frederica's landlord to toss the two of you out was the work of a moment. Consider it a warning only.*

As you have little to do with your days, the inconvenience of moving houses is, I am sure, nothing. A woman of your fortitude will find the task poses little problem. If, however, I am forced to inconvenience myself to the extent of ruining Daughtry's Bank— where your sister draws her annuity—you can rest assured I will not remain so pleasant.

My offer still stands: fifty pounds and a reference. I can, perhaps, increase the monetary compensation somewhat.

I'd rather not cause you any further disruption, but I will not hesitate, should it prove necessary.

As always, I am

Yours.

There was no signature.

Serena stared at the offending missive, anger growing in her heart. She'd been prepared to have any threat leveled at her. But to threaten Freddy once again? It was like abusing baby squirrels.

She flipped the paper over, and on the blank reverse, scrawled her response.

Cut line, sir. My sister and I have scarcely a hundred pounds to lose between the two of us. Such infinitesimal reserves will hardly be missed.

Not true, but in her experience, wealthy men never understood the value of money. She nodded fiercely at that, and then played the card that she'd been holding in abeyance for this moment.

But you know—and I know—and all of Mayfair knows—that the duchess will not be pleased if she hears my story. I am not frightened of you; how could I be? I have nothing to lose. I am already ruined.

Clermont, on the other hand… Do remind me. Is it twenty thousand pounds at stake if his wife deserts him, or forty? The gossips never get the figures clear.

I address one final thing. You are not mine, and I'll thank you not to address me in so familiar a fashion.

S. Barton

She handed her response off to the footman, who actually answered the door for her this time around, and returned to her bench—today, it was vacant. It was cold, but her rage kept her warm. And in any event, she wasn't kept waiting long. The footman brought Mr. Marshall's response out to her around noon.

Dear Serena, he had written.

She was sure he'd addressed her by her Christian name solely to irritate her.

You may pretend all you wish, but you and I both know that no matter how you protest, your resources are all that stand between you and a life on the streets. The duke, of course, might be inconvenienced by a lack of money, but he will be shielded from the true cost of poverty.

Will you?

Still yours,

Hugo.

Serena's hands had grown cold as she read, but she grabbed her pencil and scrawled a response.

I, at least, have some experience with poverty. I don't relish repeating it, but I am positive I will make do. Can your duke?

I have some tips for him on frugal living; I shall be sure to pass them along if his wife abandons him completely. Here's one: Did you know that a mixture of two parts vinegar, two parts oil, and one part treacle makes a passable lemonade?

S. Barton

It took a little more than half an hour for a response to arrive.

Serena—

The vinegar solution was actually quite disgusting, which I presume was your intent. In the interest of fairness and gentlemanly conduct—two things that I cannot pretend that I normally aspire to—I must award you the upper hand in that particular bout.

I say this in all seriousness: It would give me the greatest sorrow to destroy your future and crush your spirit.

Yours.

There was a line crossed out beneath that, so darkly that she couldn't read the original words, and then:

Postscript. I am not indifferent to your welfare, even if it seems otherwise. I can see you from my office window. It cannot be good for you to pace so frantically.

Serena swallowed, and then glanced up. The windows of Clermont House reflected the dying afternoon sun. She could see movement behind the curtains—vague shadowy figures, as of housemaids going about their duties dusting—but nobody that looked like Mr. Marshall.

I see, she wrote slowly on the reverse of his letter. *You've been watching me. If you'll look out your window now, I have a special surprise for you.*

She handed this to the butler and then stood by her bench, waiting. Her heart pounded. Her hands were clammy. God, Freddy had it right—she jumped into everything without thinking, and now look what—

Her breath caught. A figure appeared in a window on the second floor. She couldn't make out any features, just a dark silhouette. Still, he could probably see her in sunlit detail. Serena forced her lips to curve into a smile.

The Wolf of Clermont raised his hand.

Before she could lose her nerve, Serena made a fist and delivered an extremely rude gesture. He stood at the window, stock-still, before turning away.

She received his note not two minutes later. She opened it, her heart pounding. But there were only two words on the paper.

Marry me.

She stared at the page for a few moments longer, struggling to make sense of it all. He'd threatened her sister. He'd threatened her well-being. But this…this was, perhaps, the most sinister thing that he'd said.

It reminded her of the foolish, inexplicable sense of security that she felt in his presence, of the sense of attraction that pulsed between them. Those words took her most vulnerable self and made a mockery of her desires.

But then, she would not be cowed. She would *not* be vulnerable. Her child's future was at stake, and no matter what weapon Mr. Marshall leveled at her, she would not flinch.

Serena raised her chin, and scrawled her response.

I was wondering when you would start threatening me with fates worse than death. Congratulations, Mr. Marshall. I am now officially frightened.

Chapter Five

I<small>T WAS LONG PAST DARK</small> by the time Hugo left work, whistling tunelessly.

He shouldn't have felt so ridiculously pleased with himself—he still had no idea what he was going to do about Miss Barton. Still, by the time she'd bested him—for the third time!—with that snipe about fates worse than death, he'd had an enormous grin on his face. It hadn't faded, not through the hours that passed, not even though he'd needed to stay long past his usual time to finish his work.

He came out from the mews, turning onto the street, tapping his walking stick against the ground in a happy rhythm. And then he stopped.

Miss Barton was still sitting on the bench.

He'd not seen her in the dark from his window. He'd assumed she was gone. If he'd known she was still present… No. He wasn't sure what he would have done, if he'd known she was waiting in the dark where any blackguard might prey upon her. He crossed the street slowly.

"Miss Barton?" he asked, his voice low and threatening. "What are you still doing here?"

She stood at his approach. Her face was grim. "What do you think? I'm waiting to speak to you."

"Me?" He took another step toward her. "Why?"

He couldn't see her expression. The street lamp was ten feet behind him, casting her face into shadow. She started toward him, and his latent awareness of her roared to life. She was a good bit shorter than he was. The fabric of her skirts rustled in the darkness. Her strides were sure and confident; her kiss would be as certain. His skin prickled in anticipation as she came up to him, within touching distance.

Before he had a chance to think, she made a fist and punched him in the jaw.

He caught her hand before she could do it again. "Never hit a man with a closed fist," he told her.

He could feel her pulse.

"Why? Because it gives you an excuse to manhandle me?"

He let go. "Slap his face instead."

"Ha."

"It will make him take you less seriously, and then he won't be expecting it when you knee him in the groin."

She let out a surprised burst of laughter at that.

"That's better," Hugo heard himself say. "I spent my day flirting with a beautiful, maddening woman," he told her. "How was yours?"

She snorted. "I spent mine receiving cowardly threats of violence," she tossed back. "Other than that, it was just lovely."

Hugo's bright, pleasant mood grew a shade darker. "Did you, then."

"Yes," she said passionately. "And as soon as he lets down his guard, I'm going to smack some sense into the fellow who threatened me."

"Was I as bad as all that, then?" Was he *apologizing* to her for doing his work? No. Of course he wasn't. That would be ludicrous.

She set her hands on her hips. "You convinced my sister's landlord to toss her out on her ear with almost no notice. We must vacate in two days. *Two days.*"

"Have you nowhere else to go?"

"You don't understand. Were it just me, this would pose no difficulty at all. But my sister…she doesn't leave her rooms, not unless she has to. When she met me at an inn a few weeks ago, she almost fainted in the crowds. It will *kill* her to leave."

"I'm sorry," he said before he could think better of it.

Apparently, he *was* apologizing. Apparently, he even meant it.

"You *should* be."

To his horror, he heard a faint sniff. That quiet suggestion of tears was quite possibly the worst thing she could have done.

He stepped closer to her. "You're not letting me get you down, are you? I have it on the best of authority that the Wolf of Clermont is all shoulders, no neck. He doesn't deserve an inch of your sentiment."

"Make up your mind," she snapped. "Either threaten me with bodily harm or be kind to me. Don't do both. It's bewildering."

"Don't exaggerate. I threatened to destroy your livelihood. But I don't threaten women with physical violence."

"Oh?" she demanded. "How do you explain your last message, then?"

It took Hugo a moment to recall what he'd said. Those impulsive two words—he'd not even known what he meant by them.

"You cannot tell me it was a serious proposal of marriage," she said. "It was intended to intimidate. And I will *not* be intimidated."

Hugo swallowed. "Marriage—to anyone—has never entered my mind. I am not the sort of man who is destined for matrimonial bliss. I have too much I wish to do with my life to saddle myself with the expense of a wife and children. Take those words as they were intended—as my frankest expression of admiration for a worthy opponent."

"You're a clever fellow," she retorted. "Express your admiration some other way. It makes me think—" She cut off, and took a step back. "What are you doing?"

He took another step toward her. She held up her hands to ward him off. Slowly, Hugo extended his walking stick to her. "Take it," he said.

"But—"

"Stop arguing, Serena, and take it."

Her hand closed around the head, and she pulled it from him.

"That," he said, "is a weapon. If I do anything you don't like, hit me on the head. It's dark. You're unaccompanied. And I am seeing you home."

She looked up at him. "I don't understand."

He didn't, either. "Don't make too much of it." Hugo shrugged and set off down the street.

⌘ ⌘ ⌘

SERENA DIDN'T KNOW what to think as she trotted down the street beside the Wolf of Clermont, swinging his heavy walking stick. His strides were not long, but they were quick and steady, and her heart beat quickly as she kept pace with him. Her mind was whirling nearly as fast.

When they slowed to pick their way across a street, Serena tried again. "I don't understand why you're doing this."

"Yes, you do," he said, not looking at her. "You understand perfectly well what is happening. We're attracted to one other, and it's inconvenient."

She sucked in a breath.

"Don't act so surprised. If I were a greengrocer, and you the charming shopkeeper's daughter across the street, we'd be calling the banns this Sunday. Likely we'd anticipate our marriage vows while our parents looked the other way."

"I wasn't acting surprised. But you're trying to unsettle me again, and I—"

"I am not. I am as far out to sea as you are." He spoke in a rumble so deep she almost didn't notice the complaint in his voice.

Serena halted on the street corner; he turned to look at her. "If I were a footman," he said, "and you a maid, we'd know every nook, every closet where we might hide away together."

Safe, her dastardly senses whispered. *He's safe*. There was something comforting about his forthright recital—comfort with an edge that only sharpened when he took a step closer to her.

"If I were a cobbler," he said, "I'd offer you a discount on shoes."

"Now you've completely lost your mind."

"No. It would give me an excuse to measure your feet with my bare hands." His lip twitched up. "And don't think I'd stop at your toes."

She had both her hands on top of his walking stick. She felt herself lean toward him, ever so slightly.

"But you're not," she said. "You're the Wolf of Clermont, and I'm the woman you cannot drive away."

"Can't is such an unforgiving word," he said. "I prefer *do not wish to.*"

This was a man who had walked away from his family at fourteen. He had a reputation for getting what he wanted.

But there was so much more to him than the boorish drone she'd once envisioned. He had talked about crushing her hopes and dreams, but when he stood next to her, he drove away the despair she'd carried for so long.

She wanted to steal him away—not to deprive Clermont of his use, but to have him for herself.

"Don't tell me I can't," he was saying. "It implies an incapacity."

"Can't," Serena repeated with a smile. "Can't can't can't."

"Ah, now you're just taunting me." He reached out and touched the side of the walking stick. "It's a good thing *this* is between us, because otherwise I might forget that I'm not a footman. Or a cobbler." He took another step in, and he was so close now that he warmed the night air around her. It scalded her lungs.

She'd thought him safe. She was wrong; there was nothing safe about him. But he stood along the path to safety. If she could steal his loyalty for her own…

For a brief moment, a dark shadow passed over her at all that would entail.

She squelched it. Never mind how she was to accomplish it. There was no point looking down when climbing. She'd repeated the word *can't,* but after months of *can't,* she was just going to have to prove that she *could.*

She uncurled one of her hands from the walking stick and laid it against his cheek. His jaw was rough and stubbled under her touch.

His breath sucked in. "Not a good idea, Serena. I'm no simple grocer. I don't intend to marry, and even if I did, it is my *job* to thwart you."

But he didn't move back. He didn't move forward, either. He simply waited, his eyes dark in the night.

Serena let go of the walking stick; it balanced on end, momentarily, before crashing to the ground.

And then he did move, slowly, leaning those final inches toward her.

At first it was just his lips that brushed hers, warm and certain, a fleeting pressure, swiftly removed. Then he rested his hand on her hip, drawing her to him. His mouth brushed hers once more; his lips parted, nipped at hers, and then again. Her whole body warmed.

She mimicked his motion—parting her lips—only to have him take them between his own, nibbling at her. She could have lost herself in that back-and-forth—the warmth of his breath, the taste of his mouth on hers. Shockingly, overwhelmingly sweet.

She'd thought of a kiss as the passive pressing together of lips—not this exchange of caresses. She was coming to life beside him—parts she'd never paid much mind to hummed in desire. The back of her neck tingled as he drew her close. The bottoms of her feet prickled with anticipation, as he kissed her again.

He licked at her lips, and she opened her mouth in shock. And as she did, he swept his tongue inside.

That act should have disgusted her. It didn't. It felt amazing. Wonderful. She opened herself up to him, and then, tentatively, reached out her own tongue. His hands slid up her body, up the curve of her buttocks to clasp her spine. One of them caressed her arm, her elbow. And then his fingers cupped her breast. Lightly, slowly, and then, when she didn't move away—when she pressed against him—with greater firmness.

And even though she knew that touch was a dreadful liberty, it felt *right* to have him touch her there—a heated counterpoint to the play of their lips.

"Ah, Serena," he murmured. "This is *not* a good idea." But he didn't stop.

His hand slid slowly down her torso to the curve of her belly. And there his fingers came to a halt.

Serena froze. She swiftly covered his hand with hers, and just as abruptly pulled away. Her heart raced.

"What is it?" he said. His voice was husky, but his eyes narrowed. The streetlamp stood behind him, coloring his dark hair with warm tones.

And then he frowned and reached out once more—tentatively this time, and feathered his hand across her stomach. One couldn't see it, not with corsets and petticoats being what they were. But a man who was pressed up against a woman, his hand caressing her, might feel it.

"Miss Barton," he said slowly. "You have neglected to tell me something. Two somethings."

"No." She was unable to meet his eyes.

"That was your first kiss, was it not?"

She couldn't bring herself to nod. Instead, she looked away.

"You said he didn't force you."

Her mouth went dry.

He shook his head. "Setting that aside—and how I can set that aside, I do not know… In all our discussions, in all the barbs we traded, was it not *once* relevant for you to mention that you were pregnant?"

Chapter Six

HUGO WAITED FOR HER to deny the accusation.

She didn't. Instead, she leaned over and picked up his walking stick. He wasn't sure if she was simply holding it between them to signal that their truce was over, or if she intended to hit him with it and walk away.

She let out a long breath. "And here I thought you knew."

"How would I know? Magic?"

"I told Clermont," she tossed back. "I assumed that what he knew, you—"

"Whatever made you imagine that he would be forthright with me? He told me this was an employment dispute. He told me that he'd hired you to take care of his unborn child."

She raised her chin. "Well," she bit off. "The position is unpaid, and he wasn't referring to his heir. But that much was true." Her hand had crept back to cover her belly. "Why do you think I'm here now? Why do you think I've spent days standing in the park? It certainly wasn't for my own benefit. I am not going to fail my child."

"Yes, and that's the other thing. What sort of promises did the duke make to get you in bed?"

She was looking off into the distance. Her nostrils flared, and then she turned to him. "He promised not to wake the household." There was a hint of a catch in her voice.

"No."

She'd given voice to his blackest suspicions and painted them blacker still. Yet she stood out against that darkness like a blinding beacon. He already flinched from the thought of hurting a woman. But everything in him rebelled at the thought of causing harm to a mother. And by the ferocity of her words—the tell-tale touch of her fingers to her abdomen—she was that.

"He had made a few comments during the day," she continued starkly. "I tried to ignore him, although it's hard to ignore a duke who is a guest of the household. He made me uneasy, though. And then he came to my room at night." The bareness of her recital was almost worse than the words she was saying. "I told him no; he insisted. I threatened to scream, and he said that if I did, the whole household would wake and they would blame me anyway. I had just started the position. If I lost it under such circumstances, I might not have found another."

He swallowed back anger. "Why did you tell me you weren't forced?"

She shook her head in confusion. "I wasn't forced. I didn't fight him."

Hugo looked over at her. She seemed to be in earnest about the last. He wasn't so certain. What the duke had done was not punishable by law, even if she had dared to bring felony charges to the House of Lords. If she couldn't prove that she'd fought back, they would never convict him.

It didn't mean she wasn't forced. Somehow, what had happened seemed even worse than physical violence—as if Clermont had taken not only his pleasure and her future, but had robbed her of the right to believe herself blameless.

"I didn't scream," she repeated. "You tell me that you admire me as a worthy opponent. But you don't understand. The only reason I refuse to back down now is because I refuse to let my child drown in silence."

"You should have told me."

"What would it have changed?"

Everything. There was a counterpoint to his father's vicious words. It was neither loud nor insistent, but sometimes when he closed his eyes, he could remember his mother singing.

"At least I wouldn't have made you stand all day, four days running," he shot back. "I'd have understood that when you asked for *recognition,* you were not speaking solely about revenge. Tell me, Miss Barton, and tell me plainly. What is it you want?"

"I want funds enough for the future."

"You're looking for perpetual support?"

"No. That farm I told you about—I want to grow lavender, make soaps, and take them to market."

He inclined his head.

"I want my child to be able to overcome the circumstances of his birth. If he is to be a duke's son, he should have some advantages. I want him to go to Eton. Or, if she's a girl, to have a Season. Clermont is the father. He owes his child some sort of future, and I will not go away until it's secured."

Hugo exhaled and tried to imagine the duke taking responsibility. He tried to imagine the *duchess* understanding. No use; it would never happen.

He tried to imagine himself driving Serena away—but that was an even more futile prospect. He was trapped between an improbability and an unlikelihood.

He frowned. "I'll need to look into a few things," he said. "But we'll talk tomorrow—let us say at eleven in the morning. And this time I mean it. No threats—not from either of us. This is a problem."

He reached out and set his hand over hers on the walking stick. She raised her eyes to his, wide and luminous.

"I solve problems," he said.

⌘ ⌘ ⌘

FREDDY HAD BEEN IN BED when Serena arrived last evening; she was still sleeping when Serena awoke, early in the morning.

Serena was just slipping into her shoes in the entry when a querulous note sounded behind her.

"Serena? Are you sneaking out already? Where were you so late last night?"

Serena's heart skipped a beat. "Out," she said.

"Out doing what?"

"Out being…out."

There sounded the thump of feet hitting the floor, and then Freddy turned the corner. Her countenance was screwed into worried little lines.

"You arrived in someone's company," she said. "I watched you."

And she'd thought Freddy asleep. Her sister had likely been too upset to speak. There was no use denying the accusation, though, so Serena simply picked up her cloak.

"A man. Haven't men caused you enough trouble?"

"It wasn't like that."

"Don't you know how men are? It is *always* like that with them. Is that how you got in trouble? Walking out with a man after dark?" Freddy grimaced. "You've never learned your lesson."

"What lesson should I have learned?"

Freddy straightened and set her hands on her hips. "I scarcely said a word when you flaunted your problems before all of Mayfair. And now I'm being forced to vacate the home I hold dear. I am made homeless, and *you* are out at all hours of the night cavorting with men."

"I wasn't cavorting. It was the Wolf of Clermont, if you must know. I *have* to speak with him. And even if it wasn't, what do you expect me to do? Hide for the rest of my life, because something bad happened to me?"

Freddy's lips compressed.

"If you're worried about where to stay, I've a few leads on rooms. I'll have us a new place by nightfall. I was just headed out to—"

As she spoke, Freddy reached down and picked up a pair of slippers. "Us?" she said. "*We* won't have anything." And then she threw the slippers at Serena.

They were made of wool and therefore bounced ineffectually off Serena's forehead. Still, she was aghast. Mild-mannered Freddy, tossing things at her?

"How dare you?" Freddy said. "How dare you bring me into this?"

"Freddy—it's just a place to stay. We'll find a new one, just as good."

"You don't understand!" Freddy looked about the entry. "You've never understood. I have only ever had one safe place—these rooms—and now you've taken them from me."

Freddy reached down and picked up the tired valise that stood next to the table.

"Listen to yourself," Serena said. "You want me to hide, just like you do—hurt once, never risking anything else again. You won't be satisfied until you've brought me down to your level."

Freddy's eyes flashed. Her lips pressed together, and in that moment, Serena had the horrible, awful feeling of having said too much. Freddy hurled the valise at her. It traveled only a few feet, lacking the basic capabilities to sustain long flight, and landed in a discordant crumple of leather and buckles.

"Do you not understand what happened to you?" Freddy glared at her. "You suffered a fate worse than death, and still you—"

"I am alive," Serena said. "My child is alive. I intend to carry on living. Can you say that much?"

At that, Freddy swiped her hand across the side-table, tipping it over. It fell with a resounding crash.

Serena stepped forward and bent awkwardly to right the furniture. Her sister let out a sniff. "Oh, don't bother," she said crossly. "I'll clean it up. I always do clean up after your messes. You would do it wrong, anyway. Go and dally with an entire company of men. I don't care."

Chapter Seven

AT ELEVEN O'CLOCK precisely, Serena was met at her bench by a man she had never seen before. He looked precisely the sort of man she would have imagined as the Wolf of Clermont a month ago—tall and muscular, eyes set close together, neck disappearing into broad shoulders.

"Miss Barton?" he asked.

Serena stood, folding the list of housing advertisements that she'd been perusing.

"I'm to show you around the back."

She followed. It was foolish to be nervous. She'd talked with Mr. Marshall before. But not since he'd kissed her. Not since he'd discovered she was pregnant with another man's child, and he'd drawn back.

He led her around the street and into a mews in back. From there, they ducked into the servants' entrance in one of the white stone houses. The door opened onto a cellar. This he passed through swiftly, taking her up several flights of a narrow stair, and from there, into a richly carpeted hall, paintings on the walls.

All around her, the surroundings echoed wealth and generations of power—everything that had aligned itself against her. *This* was what she'd been fighting against. Not just the Duke of Clermont, or Mr. Marshall, but an entire country's worth of opinion. She was as nothing compared to this sort of power—nothing more than a single grain in an entire sack of wheat. Nobody cared whether kernels wished to be ground into flour. It didn't matter if she spoke or stayed silent; she had no voice either way.

Well, it mattered to her.

The servant came to a stop in front of a door, and Serena drew in a breath.

Her escort rapped on the door, once.

"Come in," a voice said.

The man beside her opened the door. He held it for her, expectantly, and she realized that he wasn't going to be entering with her.

She stepped into the room. Big strides. Head high. *Breathe,* she reminded herself. She was in an office—or at least she assumed it was an office. It could have been a library, with those books on the shelves. But there was paper everywhere—not only strewn about in loose stacks, but also set in cunning little shelves and tied up with different colors of cotton tape, all of which seemed to have some meaning. Blue there, yellow here, red spread out on the desk.

She couldn't see Hugo—the high back of the black leather chair was turned to shield him.

"Well, Mr. Marshall," she said, walking into the room with more bravery then she felt, "So this is where you crush hopes and shatter dreams."

"Very droll." He rose to his feet. Despite his words, there was no indication that he saw anything amusing at all. His mouth was set in one firm, sober line. And when he'd caught her attention, he gestured to the solitary wooden chair that stood across the desk from him. "Sit," he commanded.

Serena smoothed her palms over her skirt and complied.

He sank into his chair. But he didn't start the conversation. He simply steepled his fingers and looked at her silently. She wondered what he was seeing. The woman he'd kissed last night? A lady of easy virtue? Or someone else entirely?

He frowned and then pushed back in his chair. "Well," he said. "We appear to have found ourselves in a bit of a difficulty."

"You don't seem to have done too badly for yourself."

"I haven't even—" He broke off and blew out a frustrated puff of air. "Never mind. Here is what we are going to offer you."

"Who do you mean by *we?*"

Mr. Marshall ignored this. "We can't provide what you ask for—no Eton, no Season. To give that much, the duke would have to exert himself for the child. His wife would discover it, and he has too much to lose."

"Then I shall continue to sit outside his house. What do you suppose the gossip will run to once I begin to show?" She began to stand.

He slammed his hand against the table with a resounding thud. "*Wait.*"

"Don't you screech at me," Serena snapped. "Not you of all people."

He stared at her a moment and then let out a breath. "My apologies," he said stiffly. "I am rather on edge at the moment. I suspect we both are." A muscle twitched in his cheek. "We are prepared to give you your fifty pounds, and then an extra fifty beyond that. Enough for you to live on, if you manage your resources judiciously. Enough to pay for a solid education or a finishing school. It's not what you hoped for, but it is the best I can manage."

She would be a fool not to take it. Anyone would say so.

But if she agreed, she'd no doubt be setting her name to more silence—a hundred supercilious looks, a lifetime of shaking heads. And her child...he would still be some nameless, unprotected bastard.

"What about my sister?" she asked.

He waved his hand. "She may stay where she is or live with you, as is her preference. This has already been communicated to her landlord; Miss Frederica Barton knows by now that she need not leave."

She should take what he'd offered. Still, Serena met his eyes and held them. "Is that all you've got to offer? It isn't enough."

He'd been watching her the entire time. But now, for the first time, he looked away.

"As it happens, there is something else." He played with the handle of a desk drawer uneasily. "What you wanted for your child was acceptance. That will be unattainable if your child is born a bastard. Eton would have been a futile promise in any event, as the founding statutes say quite clearly that any boy who attends must be legitimate. Have you any plans to marry at present?"

"You know I haven't."

He was still looking away, addressing the desk. "Consider acquiring some."

Serena felt herself flush.

"Mr. Marshall, recall the circumstances in which I find myself. I have no great wealth, no family name to shield me. I am pregnant with another man's child. Marriage is simply not an option."

His expression did not change. "On the contrary, Miss Barton. You have a pending proposal of marriage—one you have not yet answered."

"What are you talking about? I think I would know better than you if someone had proposed."

"Think harder, Miss Barton. I know the circumstances of the offer quite well. I should. After all, I made it."

Her heart came to a standstill. That note, that confusing, heart-rending note that he'd sent her...was it just yesterday afternoon?

"That wasn't seriously meant," she protested. "You don't want to get married."

"Don't imagine it would be the usual kind of marriage." He seemed to withdraw even more. "It needn't even be consummated. Any woman I liked well enough to marry doesn't deserve to be saddled with me. If we marry, it will be a quiet wedding by special license in a back room. At the end, we'll go our separate ways—you, to your farm, and me..." He looked around the small room at the messy piles of paper. "I'm not offering to make a life with you. I am merely giving you the chance to make your child legitimate. Nothing more."

He watched her, his eyes hooded and wary. And deep inside… She had no notion as to what to say.

She let out a long breath. "Oh, you *are* romantic."

His lips compressed. "Grow accustomed to it. This is business, not romance."

He glanced down, avoiding her eyes, and sifted through papers on the desk before him. "You wanted a lease on a farm within your means, did you not? Shall I look out for properties for you, or would you like to conduct the search yourself?"

"I would hate to put you to any trouble."

"No trouble." He glanced up warily at her. "As it happens, I've already started. There are some possibilities detailed here." He rescued a sheaf of papers teetering on the edge of the desk and slid them over to her.

No; it wasn't coldness she detected in his manner. He was nervous. And if he was nervous…

Serena had never been able to suppress hope for long. It filled her now.

There were no fates worse than death. There were only temporary setbacks on the road to victory. And no matter how coldly he phrased the prospect of their marriage, one thing was quite clear. She had won.

He was hers. Not Clermont's. Not anyone else's. No matter what he said, one didn't tie oneself to a woman for life without granting her one's loyalty. She stood, ignoring the papers he'd shoved over to her.

"The key to picking a good property," he said, reaching across the desk to shuffle the pages, "is to think of where you'll have water and sunlight and to look at prior crop yields. Those will tell you much about the quality of the soil."

She stepped around the desk and set her hands on his shoulders.

He stopped. Swallowed. "Lavender—you did say lavender, did you not?—grows best in dry, sandy soils, neither alkaline nor acidic in nature. You might start looking at the properties in Cambridgeshire that's one of the driest parts of all of England, you know. Search out a soil that produces carrots on a regular basis, and…" He trailed off as she leaned toward him.

"You would be giving up all chance at marriage, Hugo. If you met someone and fell in love…"

"Will never happen. Never wanted it." He let out a shaky puff of air, and Serena realized that he had been holding his breath.

"I have no time for women." He raised his hand to her face and skimmed his fingertips down the line of her jaw, trailing them along her skin, until his index finger reached her chin. "Not even for you," he whispered.

She raised her eyes to his. "Are you telling me I can't?"

He made a confused, scalded noise—and then his arms came around her, catching her to him, pulling her down to sit on his lap. His lips were soft on hers—soft and sweet, but oh so hungry.

He'd claimed there was nothing of romance in this, but she wouldn't have known it from his kiss. It wasn't just his tightly-constrained want. A man who was driven solely by physical lust would have tried to seduce her first and marry her never. Instead, he kissed her as if it were his last time. As if she were a glass of water, and he the man about to embark on a trek across the desert. He savored her with his lips.

For a moment, she believed that no matter what he'd said, their marriage might become real. He was going to change his mind. She could taste it in his kiss.

But then he pulled away. "As you can see," he said hoarsely, "this is nothing more than selfishness on my part. There's no room for you in my life. But this way, at least I'll know that you're safe."

He was fooling himself if he thought she would settle for a half-marriage. She'd vowed to win him from Clermont. She'd be damned if she stopped with less than full victory. She'd brought him this far. He would change his mind.

"I see," Serena said softly, setting her palm against his cheek. "There's no romance at all."

"None." And this time, his eyes didn't drop from hers.

Chapter Eight

SERENA HAD LEFT HER SISTER this morning with everything between them unsettled. She hadn't known what would happen to her, what Hugo Marshall intended, and whether Freddy would ever speak to her again. And so when she pushed the door to her sister's room open, she held her breath.

Everything appeared to be back to strict order. Freddy's gloves were neatly laid atop one another on the table in the entry; her half boots, dry and unused, stood underneath. When she peered around the doorframe, there was no sign of the clothing that Freddy had flung at her, nor of the valise that had landed at her feet. It had all been packed away.

Serena stepped cautiously into the front room.

Freddy was sitting at the window, her hands full of linen that seemed far finer than the usual charity work she did. The fabric was a golden-orange, with a subtle damask pattern woven into it.

"Frederica?" Serena asked.

"There's bread in the box and fresh milk," Freddy said. "And apples—I had Jimmy bring up some apples from the green grocer. I thought we might make us a supper of that."

Jimmy was the boy who lived downstairs; Freddy paid him to fetch things. But even thirteen-year-old Jimmy was sometimes too much for Freddy. If she'd been willing to talk to him…

Serena had almost hoped that Freddy would stay angry. Instead, she was hiding behind a façade composed of the commonplace. She had already retreated inside a thick shell built from these rooms. Nothing Serena said— nor anger, nor tears—would coax her out.

"Freddy," Serena tried, "I'm sorry."

Freddy looked up from her work long enough to frown. "You should be. I've told you not to call me Freddy time and time again." She glanced down sharply and smoothed out the fabric she was working on. "It's not ladylike. I don't wish to answer to such an appellation."

"You were right. I put you at risk, and—"

"You always put things at risk. If you fell out of a tree as a child, I'd clean you up and bandage your knees, and next I looked you'd be out climbing again. You never learned your lesson."

Oh, she'd learned her lesson: *Climb harder.*

Somehow, Serena didn't think that was the lesson Freddy had expected her to learn.

"It's always the same thing," Freddy said. "You fall, I catch. And before you've even healed up properly, you're out looking for a new way to fall."

Freddy clucked her tongue disapprovingly, and Serena stared at her.

Here she'd been thinking that *Freddy* was damaged beyond repair, hiding from the world. Freddy thought that Serena was unprotected. Was that how she seemed to Freddy? Some strange, impetuous creature, launching from disaster to disaster, simply because she refused to give up? The vision this invoked of herself was so alien that Serena was robbed of a response.

How could they be sisters? It seemed impossible that they should view the world with such fundamentally different eyes.

And yet there was Freddy—*Freddy,* who hadn't stirred from these rooms since she met Serena at the inn where the stagecoach had deposited her—shaking her head as if *Serena* were the one on the brink of commitment to Bedlam.

There was no way to give voice to her thoughts.

No, Freddy. You appear to be mistaken. I am not mad; you are.

"What are you working on?" Serena finally asked instead. "That fabric's beautiful."

"It's one of Mother's old dresses," Freddy said calmly. "I'm making it over. I thought it would do for a wedding dress for you."

Serena choked. "How did you *know?*"

"I'm your sister, Serena." Freddy spoke with a smile that was as annoying as it was mysterious. "I know everything."

"No, you don't."

"Your Mr. Marshall paid me a visit this morning. Just after you left. He told me he was going to ask." Freddy pulled a face. "I suspect you're going to say yes. It's the sort of fool thing you would do—trusting your entire fate and future to some man you scarcely know, when you could stay here in perfect safety."

Safety? *Immobility* seemed a better word.

"In any event," Freddy said, "when it all falls apart, I'll be here to catch you and pick up the pieces. Again."

Freddy would never shatter. She couldn't; she'd never ascend to any great heights. One day, though, she'd come to the plodding end of her resources. She would suffocate in her tiny room.

"What if it doesn't fall apart?" Serena asked.

Freddy stared at her, her gray eyes narrowing. "How you can still ask that, when—" She exhaled deeply and rolled her eyes. "Never mind. Now are you going to try this dress on, so we can see where it needs pinning?"

There was no winning this one.

"Thank you," Serena finally said. "Help me with my buttons, please."

⌘ ⌘ ⌘

THE WEEK BEFORE THE WEDDING flew by in a frenzy of licenses and leases. Hugo found it better to keep himself busy with details, rather than ponder the impenetrable mystery of his impending nuptials.

Whenever the thought crossed his mind—*you're getting married*—he thrust it away.

Marriage was an entanglement. *This* was simply a business commitment. To a woman.

Just your everyday, average business arrangement—except this one gave him the right to take her to bed.

That was the reason why he didn't dare think about what he was doing—because once he thought of Serena Barton as his wife-to-be instead of as a partner in an arms'-length arrangement, his imagination wandered.

It wasn't the thought of bedding her—repeatedly—that most caught his fancy.

It was the thought that for the first time in years, he might have someone. Marriage became companionship. Companionship became a reason to give up his fight, to spend evenings with her instead of poring over shipping records, searching for a pattern that would yield profit.

No. He couldn't let himself dwell on that.

But not thinking about his inchoate wishes left him unprepared when he reached the church where they were to be married. He felt off balance throughout the ceremony—as if he were on the brink of stumbling and couldn't reach out to catch himself.

He couldn't bring himself to look directly at her. Her gown was the color of daylight just before sunset; if he looked at her too long, he feared he might be left blind once she was gone. The vicar stood between them, reciting words that Hugo couldn't comprehend—*richer* and *poorer, troth, wife.* He repeated his vows in a dream; he barely heard her answers.

But when he took her hand to slip his ring onto her finger, she was solid and warm—the only real thing in the room. He almost didn't want to let go of her. The vicar gave him permission and he kissed her—not hard, for lust, nor long, for love, but a light brush of his lips for the brief space of time that she would stay in his life.

In the hired carriage after, as he returned Serena and her sister to her home, he could not help but think of what he would not have. The carriage drew up; her sister disembarked.

Serena did not move.

"The lease is in order," Hugo said, "and I've arranged your passage on the stage. I hired a woman to see you through the next year. Don't argue; you shouldn't be alone under the circumstances."

She was turned away from him.

"Thank you," she said. Her hand clenched in the fabric of her skirts convulsively.

"If you need me for anything, you have only to ask." A foolish offer, but then, he was used to turning into a fool around her.

"I...that is..." Her voice quivered and deep inside, some part of him quailed.

"What?" The word came out cold, but he didn't care.

She turned to him. "I think we should consummate the marriage after all."

Yes, some possessive beast inside him growled. But what came out was the clipped version: "Why? Is this some sort of misguided thanks? I don't want—"

Her lips thinned. "Because maybe you can pretend that this is solely a business transaction, but I cannot. Consummation will provide us both with some protection, should the marriage be challenged. More than that. We are *married*—and maybe this is no conventional arrangement, but it is still *real.*"

"It isn't," he said.

"It is. What is a husband, but the man who offers you support when all the world turns you away?"

Was that what he was to her? He couldn't look at her now, or she'd see how much those words affected him.

She continued. "What is a wife, but a partner who will see you through to your deepest wishes? We have promised each other our deepest wishes."

"Have we?"

"You will be my protection from the world. And I..." She set her hand on his arm, and a prickle ran up his neck. "Legally, you're obligated by my actions. Another woman might take advantage. You've trusted me not to thwart your ambition. Let me trust you with this, too."

Yes.

He couldn't make his lips form the word. He couldn't even bring up his hands to touch her. Instead, he gripped the edge of the seat. "Have no hope of me, darling. I have none to give you."

"Liar." Her voice shook, but her hands were steady on his shoulder. And then slowly, ever so slowly, she leaned in to him. She smelled of bergamot and soap, of sunshine and sugar. He was so, so lost.

He met her lips with his own, settled his hands about her waist and drew her in. He held her close—as close as he'd wanted all these past days.

She nestled against him, her lips soft against his. He didn't want to let go. He could have kissed her forever.

Instead, the carriage door swung open.

"Guv'nor?" It was the driver. "Oh—uh—oh."

Hugo looked up, his arm full of woman.

"I don't—this isn't—" The cabbie was sputtering.

"Calm yourself," Hugo said. "We've just married." He didn't meet Serena's eyes. "Take us to Norwich Court."

Serena's hands stilled in unspoken question.

But he couldn't bring himself to make an answer. Not when he had nothing to offer.

⌘ ⌘ ⌘

THE CARRIAGE PULLED UP OUTSIDE a bleak, thin row house.

Serena had expected something more sumptuous from the man who was responsible for Clermont's fortune. But Hugo made no apology for the dark, narrow stair he led her up, nor for the haphazard disarray of the rooms beyond the door that he unlocked. There were two low openings off the main room—so low that Hugo would have to stoop to get through them.

He wasn't neat. Truthfully, after staying with Freddy, Serena suspected that *nobody* would ever seem neat again. A jacket hung on a chair; a pair of stockings was strewn across the floor.

She peered into one of the neighboring rooms and found stray barrels and a trunk. In the other was a bed—heaped haphazardly in bedclothes and tousled sheets.

Neither of them said a word.

She wasn't sure what she'd expected—that she'd offer herself to him and win him from the duke? That he'd become her husband in truth, cleaving unto her as the words of the wedding ceremony suggested he should?

But there was no cleaving. They felt awkwardly, painfully separate.

Before Serena could lose her nerve, she ducked into his bedchamber. Her heart pounded, but she unbuttoned the pelisse that covered her gown and set it over a chair, then tugged off her gloves. Her hands were shaking by the time she undid the sash on her gown, but still she started to unhook the bodice. It was foolish for her hands to shake—foolish, because she felt no trepidation.

She couldn't feel trepidation. She wouldn't let herself. As long as she didn't look down…

But she looked up from her buttons to see Hugo standing in the doorway, watching her. There was a point, she'd discovered climbing trees as a child, when she reached the end of the branches. When the leaves gave way to sun, and the breeze blew fresh and unhindered upon her face.

For a few seconds when she reached the top, she would feel the finest sense of accomplishment. But that was also the moment when she first looked at the distant ground between her feet. And when she did, what came to mind was not the thrill of victory, but: *Now how am I going to get down?*

She'd been outrunning her fears for so long, pushing them away, pretending the ground didn't exist below her. But now she'd secured her farm and saved her child from bastardy. She'd set everything else aside for later. And now, with nothing left to reach for, later had come.

He didn't move toward her, but he didn't have to. The dark recesses of her imagination took hold anyway. He was going to push himself on top of her. His weight would pin her down. She could hear herself breathing overloud; her vision darkened at the edges.

She wasn't sure where the first tear came from, or the second. She wasn't the sort of woman to do anything so useless as weep.

But the next thing she knew, she was crying into the orange linen of her wedding gown. And these were no demure, dainty tears; they were great gasping sobs that she couldn't hold back.

She wasn't sure when he came to sit next to her on the bed, when his arms went around her. When he started to wipe away her tears.

He didn't offer useless platitudes, promising that all would be well. He didn't murmur sweet nothings. He simply held her. It felt as if his warmth enfolded her for hours. When the storm began to fade to hiccoughing sobs, he handed her a clean handkerchief.

"Uncomfortable memories?" he finally asked.

Those. Impossible emotions, too. Guilt. Fear. Anger. All the things that she had put off like so many unpaid bills had returned to hammer on her door, insisting on immediate collection of all amounts owed.

Serena blew her nose. "It's nothing. Don't worry about me. Just—can you just get on with it?"

"No, sweetheart. I have to be aroused to get on with anything, and I find nothing to desire in laboring over a woman who wishes herself elsewhere." He touched her nose. She was sure it must have been red. But he didn't comment on her looks. "Even if she is you," he said.

"I'm well now."

He shook his head. "I don't think this should happen."

He started to stand, but she set her hand on his arm. "You don't understand. I only have the one memory of Clermont. I need…" She gulped air. "When I wake up at night, remembering his weight upon me, I want another memory I can hold to, so that I might banish the thought. I need you to drive him out."

She gathered all her nerve and stood. The bodice of her gown was already undone. All she had to do was slide the sleeves off her shoulders and let the fabric fall. Like that, she was left in corset and chemise.

She had hoped that disrobing would do the trick. But he was not overcome by lust at seeing her in dishabille. He simply walked to her.

He was warm against her, warm and close; he parted her hair briefly and then, pulled a hairpin free.

"We're not going to be doing this that way, Serena," he said.

She swallowed. "Which way is *that* way?" Her voice was unsteady.

He removed another hairpin. "Whichever way you're thinking of right now. Your hands are shaking."

"What—how—I don't know—" She choked on her uncertainty, on the dark fears that rose up inside her.

But he kept removing her pins, one by one, scarcely touching her as he did so. Her coiffure tilted alarmingly, and then, as he freed a particularly crucial bit of iron, her hair tumbled down to her shoulders.

"What do you intend?" she asked.

"I am not going to consummate this marriage." He found one last pin, dangling in her curls, and set this against the others that he'd gathered. He arranged them in his hand, a neat row of gray metal.

"You're not going to consummate the marriage," she repeated.

"I'm not." He held out his hand, and when she reached out to take it, he dumped the hairpins in her palm. "But you are."

The heat of his body had warmed the pins. While she was staring at them in confusion, he closed her fingers around them.

"This is how it works," he said. "You may trade a pin for a favor. If you want me to unlace your corset, you can give me a pin. If you want me to give you a kiss, it will cost you a pin. But until you ask, I can't touch you."

Serena swallowed.

"Once I have a pin from you," he said—and this time, he gave her that long, slow smile that she remembered so well—"I can trade it back."

"For a favor?" Her voice was still shaking. "You could trade a pin for the right to—"

"Ah, yes. You can make me touch you. But I can only make you touch yourself."

"That hardly seems fair."

His smile quirked up at one end. "I'm not known for fairness."

Safe. Safe. It was coming back, that impulse—slowing her heart, driving her darkest fears from the odd corners of her body. He didn't move. The dark images that had begun to infest her slowly dissipated. And in their place was...confusion.

Still, she knew where to start.

"Take off your coat." Her voice shook as she did.

He held out his hand. "A pin, please." She handed one over. Her fingers brushed his palm as she did.

He undid the buttons down his front and then shrugged out of the dark brown material in one smooth motion. His shirt was white underneath; it clung briefly to muscle as he wrestled his coat to the side. He let it fall to the floor in an untidy mess, and turned to face her in his shirtsleeves. Somehow, taking off that outer layer made him seem bigger than before—perhaps because all that impressive breadth of shoulder was that much closer to her.

Serena's pulse beat harder, but still he didn't move.

"Aren't you going to ask for anything with your pin?" she finally managed.

"No," he said, with infinite casualness. "I want to build up a store of them first." He didn't elaborate, but her breath caught. Not, this time, in trepidation. No; this time she felt the first tendrils of curiosity curling about her.

She pointed a pin at him. "Your waistcoat, then, if you please."

He complied. She couldn't see through the linen of his shirt, but she could make out the form of his muscles as he worked—strong, defined curves.

She was growing braver now, and handed him another pin when he finished. "Your shirt."

Wordlessly, he doffed that. As he pulled the fabric over his head, the muscles of his chest flexed and rippled, and Serena stared. She'd known he was a pugilist—his shoulders *were* broad—but there was nothing quite like seeing the truth of his former profession laid out in the flesh. Those shoulders had tensed when he'd struck another man. He'd taken blows against the hard ridges of his belly. A faint, pink scar traveled in a curving line up from his navel to halfway up his chest; a more ragged red line marked his ribs. There was an entire story written in his skin, and she wanted to learn it all.

He hadn't said anything as she looked him over, but he was hardly unaware of her perusal.

"Are you flexing your muscles for me?" she asked.

"That," he said smoothly, "would be vanity."

She felt herself smile in response—the first smile since she'd entered his room. "So, yes, then."

He gave her a darkly wicked grin. "Should have known better than to try to bamboozle the governess."

Serena took a step toward him, and his smile froze. She reached out and touched the point of the pin to his abdomen. His breath stopped. She trailed it up his ribs, and had the pleasure of seeing him break out in gooseflesh.

"I want your shoes." Her mouth was dry; she could scarcely swallow around the words.

He bent to remove them. As he did, his trousers grew tight around his buttocks, and the muscles in his behind shivered.

So did she. She waited until he straightened before handing him another pin. "Do it again. I want your stockings."

This time, when he bent, he showed off for her—turning at an angle, flexing precisely *so*. He had to know how his thighs looked with all that wool hugging them. He didn't say a word, but when he'd discarded the knit wool of his stockings, he met her eyes and winked.

He'd made a game with the pins, one that stole her dread away. Still, she handed him another hairpin. "Do you have enough yet for your nefarious plan?"

"Not quite." He grinned. "Besides, you're doing so well on your own. I'd hate to interrupt you."

Her confidence was coming back. Serena tapped him on the chin with a head of a pin. "For that impertinence, sir, I demand your belt."

"You demand it, do you?" He set his hands on the buckle, and tightened it. "Then I suppose I am bound to comply." The tongue of the belt came loose, and then he pulled the belt slowly away. His trousers slipped down his hips a few inches as he did, revealing a dark arrow of hair, dotting down the front of his stomach.

She wanted to know where that trail of coarse hair led.

"Now," she began, "I want—"

"*Now,*" he interrupted smoothly, "it's time for me to redeem my pins." He fixed her with a steady look.

It was only a moment that he looked into her eyes—half a second, scarcely even long enough to blink—but already her pulse jumped in response. His smile broadened. Her skin tingled. She was aware of every inch of her skin—her shift scarcely covered her limbs; her corset bound her breasts tightly. She wasn't sure if it was fear or arousal that had her so suddenly on edge.

"My first order." He set a pin in the palm of her hand. "Wait right there until I come back."

She blinked, but he ducked out of the room before she could gather breath to protest. She took one step forward, before remembering that he'd asked with a pin, and under the rules of the game, she couldn't follow. But he didn't return—not for several minutes. She heard the clanking of metal and the working of a bellows—what in God's name was he doing? Eventually, there was a hiss like steam and his muffled oath.

He finally returned bearing a towel. A steaming towel.

"This is a trick," he said. "I learned it prize-fighting. Lie down on the bed."

At that bare command, Serena froze. He paused and cocked his head, and then set a pin on the table beside her. "I'm not touching you—recall that I can't until you ask. Lie down on the bed."

Serena swallowed and complied. He sat next to her; the mattress gave way beneath his weight.

"Put this over your face."

He handed over the cloth, hot and moist—almost too hot to touch. She unfolded it gingerly and then laid it over her eyes, covering her nose.

"Breathe in," he said. "Slowly, now."

The air was humid; she could feel the heat penetrating her skin, relaxing muscles she had not realized she'd tensed.

"Now exhale." She did; the air beneath the towel cooled temporarily. "Inhale."

She was drifting away on warmth with every breath. "This is lovely."

"Yes," he said. "The more limber you are before a fight, the less likely you are to be hurt. Don't know why that would be, but I suspect the same might hold true here as well."

She let out a little sigh of contentment. "What now?"

"I couldn't say," he replied. "I'm out of pins."

She pulled the towel from her face. "How can that be?"

He was watching her intently—his eyes dark, his mouth set in a determined line. He gestured to the table where he'd been laying pins the whole time. "I told you to breathe."

She had thought that lust would be selfish, no matter who entertained it. But there was a decided lift to his chin, a look in his eyes. He'd done all that for her—to steal the tension from her muscles, the fear from her heart.

She *was* safe. This was the man she'd come to know. Determined, yes, and ambitious, too. But also playful and kind. He hadn't hurt her. He'd seen her distress and he'd soothed it away.

She pushed one of the pins he'd piled up over to his side and took a deep breath for courage. "Take off my corset, Hugo."

He'd scarcely touched her since he'd taken her hair down—just the brush of his fingers against hers as the pins had changed ownership.

He touched her now, curling one hand around her hip. His other rose to address the knot of her front-lacing corset. He loosened the garment almost reverently. His fingertips seemed almost to scorch her, even through the stiff fabric of her undergarment. Her lungs caught fire as he loosened the laces. She took a deep breath and inhaled his smell—something like salt and citrus.

Slowly, he undid the fastenings, peeling her corset from her. Released from confinement, her breasts swelled out in front of her, covered only by the thin fabric of her chemise. The air was cool against her skin, but she could scarcely feel it.

His breathing had grown ragged. His gaze rested on the swell of her breasts, where her nipples made sharp peaks in the linen of her undergarment. His eyes moved in time with the cycle of her breath—up and down, as if he were already joined with her on some level.

He slid her pin back to lie next to the others. "Touch your breasts."

His voice was rough; his words sent a current of heat through her. She brought her hand up, never taking her eyes from his. She cupped the curve of one breast in the palm of her hand and his pupils dilated. She ran her thumb along the upper slope and he licked his lips. Her own touch sent a weak spark of pleasure pulsing through her, but it was his gaze—worshipful, almost devout—that magnified the thread of pleasure, encouraging it to grow.

She made another circle with her thumb, and he drew in another breath. And then, because her body begged for it—because his eyes pleaded for it— she teased her nipple with her fingertips. Desire shot through her, taking up an insistent, liquid beat between her legs.

He didn't move to touch, to take. He just watched, his breath growing ragged. Her pleasure was his.

"Now..." She swallowed, and gathered her nerve. "Now you touch my breasts."

He leaned over her, setting his warm hand where hers had been. His thumb was rougher and more callused, brushing her nipple through the fabric of her shift. If her own touch had brought on a shock of pleasure, his called up a rough well of desire, dark and needy, from deep within. He leaned down and touched his lips to her other nipple. His breath was hot and humid; his tongue outlined the dark, puckered skin. She gave herself over to the sensation of being touched by him—small caresses still urgent with want; tongue and then teeth, teasing her, bringing her to the edge of her want.

"Stop," she panted.

He pulled away. The muscles of his arm strained, holding himself in place.

"I want your trousers," she told him.

"I want your chemise."

They'd stopped exchanging pins, Serena realized—just slipped into one request given for another. She took a deep breath and pulled her chemise over her head. She freed her arms just in time to see him kicking his trousers and undergarments away. Now she could follow that dark line etched on his belly all the way down to a curly nest of hair, from which jutted his erection. He was hard and long, and so thick her fingers would scarcely meet if she were to place her hand around his member.

She reached out experimentally—yes—her thumb just overlapped her forefinger. He hissed as she touched him, but did not otherwise move. She stroked down his length, wondering at the contrast—warm and soft at first touch, yet hard as steel when she squeezed him. He made a noise in the back of his throat, something akin to a growl, and his hands gripped the bed sheets, but he didn't move. He didn't kiss her. He didn't take her in his arms. He simply shut his eyes and let her explore.

She let go of his erection and ran her hands up his body: up the rippling muscles of his abdomen, up the expanse of his chest. She rested her hands on his shoulders and then pushed onto her knees and kissed him.

As she did, she stretched out against him full-length. All that warm skin, all that hard muscle pressed flush against her body.

His mouth took hers with bruising force. Her tongue darted out to his, and he met her, stroke for stroke, kiss for kiss. She felt herself turning to liquid, each heated kiss stoking a building fire. But still he didn't wrap his arms around her.

She closed her hand around his member once more and he jerked almost spasmodically. "Ah, sweet—" he said, low and hoarse. She burned all over, from head to foot. But pressing herself against his hardness wasn't enough. She needed more—needed his arms around her, his body demanding more of her. She wasn't sure when her bravado had turned into brazenness.

"Touch my breasts again," she said.

The command was less shy; his response was more certain. He set his hands on her waist and slid them up her ribs to cup her naked breasts. No teasing caress, now; he leaned to kiss one, then the other—first just lips touching, and then the entirety of his mouth, hot, his tongue stroking her nipple. So good—he felt so good.

Her thighs began to tremble; he sank to sit on the bed, and pulled her to straddle him. That put her breasts right in front of him, and he took them again, tasting them. His hard erection fitted against the juncture of her thighs. Her want had gone beyond the tingle of her skin. It swelled to fill her all over. She was wet between her legs. She shifted against him, sliding against his hardness, and her desire intensified.

Again. Again. She rose up on him to press once more, and the head of his member pushed into place. She opened her eyes to regard him. His hand found hers; their fingers tangled.

He didn't say anything. He didn't have to. Her limbs seemed to melt. She could not hold herself in place, poised as she was.

And so she let go, relaxing the muscles that held her over him. She simply let herself sink onto his length. He was so big inside her. But the sensation wasn't unpleasant. It was…lovely.

She was *safe*. Safe to simply experience the hardness of him, the stretch of her body, the growing pulse of her desire. It was safe to want—to rise up on her knees and then engulf him once more.

Their eyes met as she did; he let out a breath, long and deep, and his hands clenched around hers.

Her body knew what to do without any need for instruction. Deep instinct led her to grind against his pelvis, to search out the right rhythm, the right friction. She lost herself in the feel of *them*—in the subtle satisfaction that swept over her at the look on his face as she moved faster.

"You lovely thing," he growled.

Passion built until it became an immense pressure, demanding release. She tried and tried, but no matter how she reached for it, it eluded her. Just when her want hit the edge of splintering frustration, he slid his hand between her legs and stroked her right where she needed it.

His touch was sure and unerring. The heat that had built released all at once, an inferno engulfing her from head to toe. She lost sight of everything but the pleasure that raged through her.

And then, when the whirlwind had passed, his hands fell on her hips and he drove into her from beneath, hammering home the echoes of her pleasure with his own. He let out a hoarse cry while she was still shuddering in the aftermath of her orgasm.

They sank to the mattress afterward. His arms came around her, warm and comforting. This was *right*—precisely what she'd needed.

He cupped her cheek.

It was a moment of precious, perfect togetherness. No wonder they referred to the act as *intimacy*. She had never felt so closely entangled with anyone before. His breaths were hers. His body…

She opened her eyes and looked into his dark gaze.

He wasn't smiling at her. If anything, his intensity had grown. "There now," he said softly. "*Now* you understand why I didn't want to consummate the marriage."

Chapter Nine

SHE HAD BEEN ALMOST LIQUID, molded against Hugo's chest. But he had no sooner spoken then all the tension crept back into her limbs. She stiffened atop him, then pulled away.

"Hugo. It doesn't have to be—"

He set his fingers across her lips before she could give voice to his deepest wants. "It does."

"That meant something to you. Something real."

"Of course it did." He sat up and took her hand. "I won't tell falsehoods about this. What we have is a species of love."

She let out a breath in surprise.

"A transitory, short-lived one," he explained. "A perfect sunrise—seen once, remembered always. Never duplicated."

"Never duplicated?" Her fingers bit into his. "Why ever not?"

"Because tomorrow you'll go to your farm. And I—"

"It doesn't have to be that way." Her hair was in wild, chestnut disarray around her shoulders and her eyes were wide and gray.

Hugo moved a lock of her hair aside. "You can't stay with me, Serena." His words sounded harsh. "Recall who I work for."

She blanched, but hesitated only a moment before raising her chin. "You could—"

"I could what? Come with you? I suppose I could, at that. But I won't. I have five hundred pounds waiting on the outcome of this affair with the duke. That's the only chance a pugilist like me has to come into that much money. With that, I can truly become someone. If I go with you—"

"You *are* someone." She frowned.

You'll never amount to anything. Hugo let out a breath. "Not enough."

"You are. Hugo, if you'd only—"

"It's not enough," he repeated grimly. He pushed away from her and swung his feet over the edge of the bed. "Do you hear? It's not enough for me."

"Not enough *what?*"

Such a reasonable question.

"Because you're intelligent and successful," Serena was saying, "and you're a good man. That thing with the pins—it was lovely. You have a way of putting me at ease."

"That's nothing," he said. "My mother was always doing things like that for me. She gave me a magic rock when I was young, and told me if I slept with it under my pillow, nothing would happen on the next day that I couldn't bear."

Beside him, Serena sucked in a breath. But he wasn't ashamed of telling her the truth. He had suffered through days that had made him doubt his mother's stone.

He brushed those memories away. "When I was older, she took an old pickle jar to the park. She told me to fill it with all the most important things. Then she buried it deep, deep, where my father couldn't find it no matter what he did."

It had been drizzling, but he'd scarcely felt the wet.

Do you have a jar, Mama?

She'd smiled and shook her head.

We should make one for you.

Her smile had fixed in place. Then she'd let out a sigh. *I've buried too many children,* she'd finally said. *I'm not burying anything else that matters. Never again.*

"Your mother sounds like a lovely woman," Serena said beside him.

"My mother told me I would be somebody." It had been reflexive soothing on her part—sheer contradiction after his father's tirades.

"Maybe you should listen to her."

You can be anyone, she'd told him, over and over.

A rich man? he'd asked.

The richest coal miner's son in all of England, she promised.

"When I left home," he finally said, "I was fourteen. I'd gone into the mines for the first time three days before, and there had been an accident. A little cave-in, nothing serious, but I was caught in the dark for five hours with nothing to do but imagine my air slowly being used up. After I got out, I said I wasn't going back." He inhaled. "My father disagreed. He broke my nose and three ribs with a broomstick. He told me I wasn't good enough, that I'd never amount to anything."

"Oh, Hugo." Her hand rose to trace along his jaw. "You can't still believe him—not after all these years."

He shook his head. "I got away because my mother stepped in—drawing my father's anger down on her. The last thing I remember, scrambling out the door, is the sound of her screams."

Her arm crept around him. "Oh, Hugo," she repeated.

"She passed away a few weeks later." He could scarcely draw breath. "So it's not enough yet, what I've managed." He balled his hands. "It's not enough to make up for leaving her. She could not have lost so much for a mere nobody."

He'd gone back to the park when he'd heard the news, and dug for that jar.

I'm going to be the richest coal miner's son in all England, he'd promised the grubby glass. And then he'd buried it again where she'd once left it—and hidden his other desires so deep that even Serena could not unearth them.

"And so that's where we are." He put his arm around her and inhaled the sweet, lingering scent of her perfume. "You can't stay. I won't leave. And now we both know precisely what it is we're giving up. It wasn't a good idea."

She let out a breath.

"But you'll be safe and you'll be well." He kissed her forehead lightly. "And that will be enough."

⌘　⌘　⌘

THE STORY, SERENA BELIEVED, would go like this: Hugo would change his mind.

She first believed he would change it when he woke up next to her, blinking away his morning bleariness. And yet he didn't.

Next she told herself he'd wash his insistence on their separation away with soap and water, or scrape it off alongside the bristles he'd acquired overnight.

He didn't; he washed and shaved and changed his clothing without once altering his decision.

He would change his mind, Serena decided, in the hack he'd hire to deliver her to the stagecoach yard.

But he said only a few words on the journey—just enough to deliver a quiet greeting when they stopped along the way for Freddy. The three of them traveled in unspeaking silence—Freddy clutching the strap, her gloves wrinkling under the ferocity of her grip, even though their conveyance scarcely swayed.

When they arrived, he made no attempt to purchase passage for himself. Instead, Hugo stood back, pretending to busy himself with Serena's trunk so that the sisters might speak.

"Well." Freddy peered around the crowded yard of the inn with a deeply suspicious look, frowning at the ostlers. "I suppose you have to thrust yourself out there, do you not?" She punctuated the end of this sentence with a deep, speaking sigh.

"Yes. I must."

"You always were an unnatural thing." Freddy raised a handkerchief to her nose as if she could blot the horses from her senses. "Still, I'll miss you. Things can be rather dull when you're not present."

Serena hugged her sister. "Take care," she said.

Freddy embraced her in return. "I always do. It's you I worry about."

Maybe Freddy would always think Serena strangely broken, and Serena would always cringe, thinking of her sister ensconced in her rooms, slowly turning to stone. There was no convincing one another, no *understanding* one another.

But when Serena had most needed it, her sister had given her a place to stay. For all that Freddy made her stomach hurt, they still shared an affection made bittersweet by all that divided them. Perhaps God gave one sisters to teach one to love the inexplicable.

"Be well," Serena said. "And go straight home, do you hear? No waiting around until the coach is out of sight."

Freddy sniffed at that and didn't answer, but she was pale and perspiring.

And then Serena turned her attention to Hugo.

His posture was forbidding—arms crossed as if to bar her way forward, his lips thinned in disapproval. There was almost no sign of the man who'd smiled and made her feel so easy—so *wonderful*—on the previous evening.

"Hugo," she said. Even his Christian name sounded needlessly formal. *Now* was the time for him to change his mind—now, as the driver called out for the passengers to board.

"Serena." His voice was as off-putting as his stance, but his eyes...oh, his eyes. He drank her in, as if he could gather her up.

He was going to say it. He was going to ask her not to leave.

But instead of telling her that he couldn't live without her—"Farewell," he said.

And then, before she could fumble for the right words—the words that would bridge the gap between the two of them and make this stunted marriage whole—he hefted her trunk with one hand and handed it into the boot of the coach. "Farewell," he repeated.

She boarded in a daze, refusing to let her confusion and numbness set in. This *wouldn't* happen. It couldn't. She fought her way to a seat near the door so that she could make out his form. He was bent over her sister, saying something she could not hear over the din of the other passengers.

Freddy actually smiled in response.

It would happen now. He would turn and see her. He *had* to. She set her fingers on the handle of the door.

Don't walk away. Her eyes clouded with tears. *You can't walk away. I love you.*

It was a revelation. She didn't know where it had come from. She only knew that it meant he couldn't walk away. He'd look over and see her, and then he'd realize that he loved her, too.

But in the end, that wasn't what happened. He didn't look up. He didn't see her. He didn't love her. He simply offered Freddy his arm. They turned, and the two of them vanished into the crowd.

Like that, he was gone.

Chapter Ten

IN THE DAYS THAT FOLLOWED Serena's departure, Hugo struggled to find normalcy. He failed. It was almost impossible to care about the details of the duke's finances. Food lost its savor. And all too often, he found himself standing by the window in his office—not working, not thinking, just staring at the empty iron bench in the square.

On the third day, he decided that speculation over how she was doing was likely distracting him, and he resolved to write her a simple letter. But when he started, he found that his pen did not obey.

Miss Barton, he wrote.

I spent my day as I normally spend my days: threatening suppliers, bullying those who are not in line with my expectations, and generally creating havoc in the lives of others. The square across the street is empty of all but the pigeons. I find myself resenting them.

He stopped and stared at the paper. Too revealing. Too friendly. And more importantly... There was that all-too-annoying error he'd made in the salutation. He crumpled it up and tossed it into the waste bin and started over.

Mrs. Marshall, he started, and found a grim satisfaction in addressing her with his name. *I hope that you are settling into your new home, and that all is to your satisfaction. Do please let me know if anything is amiss, and I shall see to it.*

He signed this, sealed it, and before he could think better of it, had it posted.

He tried not to think of her in the coming days, but it was rather like trying not to think of an elephant: One couldn't tell oneself not to think of elephants without bringing to mind large, gray creatures.

Her reply came a few days later.

Mr. Marshall, she wrote. *My new home is all that I had hoped for. Everything is to my satisfaction. Nothing is amiss. Thank you very much for your concern.*

He stared at those words in frustration. There was absolutely nothing to respond to there—nothing he could say without volunteering his own unsettled thoughts or asking questions that might reveal feelings that he was better off not sharing.

They'd married. He'd chosen to do without her. Anything else he might communicate would just hurt them both more. The best thing for all would be to keep this perfunctory—an occasional letter, from month to month, just to see how she fared.

And yet when he left work that evening, he didn't go directly to his home. He found himself meandering about the streets. Everywhere he looked, he saw couples together. Husbands and wives, seated next to each other in open barouches; young courting couples, sending one another flirtatious glances. Everyone was pairing up like turtledoves in the autumn chill. Only he was alone.

He'd never cared about such a thing before. He wasn't the sort to dwell on what *wasn't*. But truthfully, it was easier to think of Serena—who was no longer in his life—than to contemplate the Duke of Clermont—who was.

He found himself standing in front of a shop, staring at a sky-blue silk shawl, wondering how it would look against her skin. And then, to his great amazement, he found himself purchasing it. He watched himself in bemusement. Had he really come to this?

When he finally made his way home in the deep darkness, he found himself sitting at his desk and dipping his steel nib in the ink once again.

Mrs. Marshall, he inscribed. *I am delighted that your new home is what you wished for, and that everything is as you've hoped. Please accept my best wishes for your happiness.*

He didn't send the shawl. He couldn't think of a way to do it—what, admit that he was thinking of her? That would have been the height of foolishness. The last thing he needed was to mislead her into believing that he would make a proper husband. It wouldn't be kind to raise false hopes—not in her, and certainly not in himself.

But perhaps she sensed it anyway, because a few days after that, he received her next response.

Mr. Marshall, she wrote, *I am delighted that you are delighted that I am delighted with my new home. Can I predict the substance of your next missive? That you are delighted that I am delighted that you are delighted, et cetera.*

I have just saved us both a great deal of postage and awkward conversation. If we keep this up, we shall quickly run through our ink. And so I shall say this as simply as I can, without once hinting that I expect any more of you. I am glad—damnably glad—that I had one night with you. There are dark times in the evening when I imagine your arms around me. For all you claim to be ruthless, you have been my shining, guiding star. Let us not pretend that we mean nothing to one another. We may not be husband and wife in the truest sense, but we have been friends and we have been lovers, and I hope that we may be friends still.

His lungs ached when he read that. His entire body ached, truth be told, from his toes to his heart.

Still, the next morning, he spent an immense sum shipping the shawl to New Shaling, along with a note: *Bought this a few days ago. It made me think of you.*

His days passed by rote. Everything was now falling into place. He'd had a message from the duke, indicating that he'd managed to smooth things over with his recalcitrant wife. Investments were coming through. In three months' time, with the duchess's revenue finally secured, he'd have made the duke more than a thousand pounds—more than five thousand pounds. He'd win his wager. From there, he'd begin to expand his empire.

The problem was that his heart wasn't in it any longer. He'd spent his entire life focused on making something of himself: on the thought that he might one day argue his father's voice into silence.

That evening, before he'd heard back from her about the shawl, he wrote to her again: *You can call me your friend if you like, but I think of you when I stroke myself. When last I checked, that points to feelings that are decidedly more than friendly. Have I horrified you too much?*

He waited days for her reply. When it finally came he read it instantly: *Sir: I am a respectable married woman. I cannot express in words the horror and revulsion that arise in me upon reading the sentiments you have communicated.*

Hugo raised his head from the letter. But he hadn't finished, and some penchant for punishment forced him to continue: *Your letter only underscored my own failings. After all, as your wife, it is my duty to stroke you. Is it not?"*

It was all Hugo could do not to leave for New Shaling on the spot.

⌘　⌘　⌘

THE HOUSE WAS BUSTLING in preparation for the duke's return. Hugo couldn't find it in him to care about much of anything. He could scarcely make himself bother over even the basics of the accounts; he didn't want to think of the future.

It was Clermont's fault—all of it. These last months had robbed him of his certainty. And what he'd taken from Serena…

Hugo shook his head. It didn't matter. He had only a few months to go. If he could stomach that, he'd win his wager, collect his money, and never see the man again.

He heard the carriage arrive below. All the other servants must have gone down to greet their master; Hugo stayed up in the office, sorting through bills and payments, reports from estates. It seemed rather ironic that even though Hugo had almost stopped exerting himself, everything prospered. Ships had come in ahead of schedule, bearing cargo that was vastly more valuable than what had been paid on the other end. The price of wheat was rising; wool was doing even better.

It was as if the entire universe was rewarding him. If this luck held up once Hugo started investing his own money, he'd be a wealthy man by the age of forty. He'd have servants and his own estate. He would beat back that dark, dismal voice inside of him by the sheer dint of his accomplishment. Perhaps in ten years, he might make another visit to New Shaling, and see if he could rekindle...

No. No. He couldn't think that way.

It took hours for the duke to recover from his journey—eating and cleansing himself, or whatever it was that dukes did after retrieving their errant wives. Hugo sat in his office, waiting for the duke to show his face. He wasn't sure if he wanted to confront him about his lies, or if he hoped the man kept away, so he didn't have to look at him.

Eventually, the man wandered into Hugo's office.

The Duke of Clermont hadn't changed. He was still a big, solid mass of a man. He hadn't grown any fatter; his eyes weren't any narrower. And yet Hugo's first thought was that the man seemed a hundred times more swinish.

"I see the governess is gone," he said cheerily. "And the duchess is back, and in a few months, assuming all is well, I'll have another payment from the trust."

"Yes," Hugo said tersely. "Good."

But the duke was in a voluble mood today. "What do you think I should buy, first thing?" he mused. "Horses? Or a mistress?"

He couldn't believe the man was still talking that way—not after all he'd been through.

"I have a better idea," Hugo heard himself say. "You could go on a journey."

"A journey? Now, there's a capital idea for escaping my wife. Brighton, perhaps? Or France?"

"None of those," Hugo said. "I was thinking that you could go to hell."

He didn't curse. He *didn't*. And yet he could not make himself regret those words. A fierce sense of rightness beat in his chest, alongside his awakening heart.

His pronouncement was met with flat silence. Clermont cocked his head in disbelief, and then slowly—ever so slowly—shook it. "I'm not—I'm rather certain"—he spluttered—"I don't believe you should address me in that fashion."

Hugo stood. He wasn't taller than the duke, but still the other man took a step back.

"You told me that you wanted me to take care of an employment matter. An *employment matter*. Do you have any idea what I might have done to her?"

"Oh, come now, Marshall. You're not going and getting a conscience on me, are you?" Clermont pouted. "It's so inconvenient, and I've had to listen to Her Grace harping on and on for the last three weeks about this and that and *morals* and *love*. My head is sick of nodding to the tune of nonsense. I have had nothing but lectures for days and days now. Is it never going to end?"

Hugo gritted his teeth. If he wanted those five hundred pounds, he had to work with this man for the next few months. He *had* to.

He clenched his hands and stood, turning away.

That sense of his own worthlessness had wormed its way under his skin until he believed it. In his mind's eye, he saw the silhouette of his father looming over him. He felt the solid weight of the broom smashing into his ribs.

You'll never make anything of yourself, you useless bloody bastard.

"There," Clermont was saying behind him, "I'm the better person. I'll forgive you for that unkind remark, and you'll forgive me for my little falsehood—and we'll be even, won't we?"

He'd never been able to get those words out of his head; his mother's intervention had driven them deep into his flesh, buried them where he couldn't touch them.

You'll never amount to anything.

And because of that, he was...what, going to walk away from the woman he loved?

No.

All the logic in the world could not stand up to one fact: He simply could not stomach Clermont's presence any longer.

"We're not even," he said in a surprisingly calm voice. He turned back around.

Clermont was watching him with those ice-blue eyes of his—clear, and yet all too confused.

"We are not anywhere near even. Tell me what you did to her—admit it aloud, you coward."

Clermont licked his lips in confusion. "She wanted it."

Hugo reached out and grabbed the other man by the collar.

"The truth, Clermont."

"She was a hot little—"

He hit the man in the stomach. He didn't bother to pull the punch, and Clermont, who had likely never been struck before in his life, went green.

There was a time for subtlety. There was a time to hold back his anger. But right now, he couldn't see the point of it.

"The truth, Clermont, or next time, I'll rip your stones out with my bare hands."

The duke whimpered. "I was so bored, and she was the closest thing to a woman around. What would it hurt?"

Hugo struck him again.

"What was that for? I'm telling the truth, now!"

"That wasn't for what you said. It was for what you did." Hugo let the man go, but only long enough to grab a piece of paper and a pen and set it in front of him. "I want you to admit that on paper."

"On paper? But—"

"On paper," Hugo said. "I want you to write on paper that you forced her to it, and that in reparation for your crime, you agree that you will send your son to Eton—or sponsor your daughter for a Season."

"But—"

"Do it," Hugo said, with every ounce of menace he could muster. "And stop sniveling about it, you worthless buffoon. Think for one second about what I know about you—what I could do to you. You more than anyone know what I'm capable of. This lets you off rather easily. If you keep your end of the bargain, the paper need never be made public. If you don't…"

He could see the duke making his sordid calculation. If the duchess found out… There were, after all, forty thousand pounds on the line. Perhaps, Hugo imagined the duke thinking with his typical cowardice, he might keep the whole thing quiet long enough to fool his wife and guarantee himself funds for years to come.

With a nod, the other man reached for the paper and wrote his confession. When he was done, Hugo sanded it carefully and folded it in half.

"If you think that I'll honor our wager after this…" the duke threatened.

Hugo walked to the door. "I have no doubts about that," he said frostily. "But then, you'll have no need to honor the wager."

"Why would that be?"

Hugo gave him one last wolfish smile and brandished the paper. "Because you'd have to be in funds for me to win. I promised I wouldn't make this paper public. I didn't promise not to show Her Grace. I think you've lied to quite enough women."

Fear shot into the duke's eyes. "Oh, God. Wait. Marshall!"

But Hugo was already through the door.

Chapter Eleven

IN THE END, HUGO COULDN'T bring himself to go directly to New Shaling. It added almost a week to his journey, but first he went north to the place of his birth and tracked down the parish records.

His father had passed away almost a decade ago, but Hugo didn't bother to find where he had been laid. Better to let him pass out of memory. He'd let the man linger on too long as it was.

He visited the park where he'd buried his jar. But fifteen years later, there was nothing to be found—only shards of glass and tree roots. Fitting.

Instead, he tracked down an unmarked stone outside a tiny church and pulled the weeds off his mother's grave. She'd had the right of it, all those years ago. You buried the dead and cared for the living.

As for the living… Three of his sisters had survived to adulthood. Of those, two had left for America; the third had simply disappeared. Out of sixteen children, Hugo was the only one who remained. All these years, he'd hefted his ambition like a heavy burden. He'd been wrong. He had been given a tremendous gift, one that he didn't plan to squander. Even though the trees had lost all their leaves and frost was beginning to nip at the fields, it felt like spring had come.

The coach that took him to Cambridge was advertised as swift, but it seemed to dawdle endlessly along the way. A cart took him the rest of the way to Serena's land.

The farm was small—scarcely two acres in size. He'd seen the maps and the markings when he'd helped Serena finalize the lease, but this was the first time that Hugo had seen the property in person. He stood back on the road a ways, wondering about his welcome. There was a single field off to the side, planted for now with winter wheat. But he could sketch in the improvements that she'd talked about building—a shed, where she might isolate and extract the essence of lavender, a coop with a gaggle of chickens, and a kitchen-garden, over by that patch of weeds just behind the house.

As he watched, the door opened, and she walked swiftly out to the well that stood on the right side of the property. He could see her pregnancy now—it was all too obvious in the way that she moved, in the slight curve of her stomach. He caught his breath.

God, he'd missed her.

She tossed the bucket in the well and then began to draw it up. She was wearing a sky-blue shawl—a familiar sky-blue shawl. The ends flapped in the breeze.

Hugo found himself crossing the road slowly, coming up behind her. "Nice shawl," he remarked.

She let out a little shriek and dropped the chain; a splash sounded, as the bucket plummeted to the bottom of the well.

"Good Lord," she said. "Hugo. Whatever are you doing here?"

He met her eyes. "What do you think?"

"I...I think..."

"I'm here to horrify you," he said. And then, because he couldn't bear it any longer, he reached out and pulled her to him. She was warm and soft in his arms, and she smelled so deliciously *right*. He could have inhaled her scent for hours.

"Hugo—"

He didn't want to talk. He didn't want to answer any questions. He didn't know who he was or what he wanted or what dreams would come to fill his heart. He only knew that if he couldn't have her, nothing would ever be right again. And so he kissed her. He tasted her, sweet and steady against him, put his hand in the small of her back and drew her toward him.

She kissed him back.

"I love you," he said. The truth took root inside him. For the first time in years, the dark words of his past receded.

"But, Hugo..."

He set his fingers over her lips. "Let me do this," he said. "I thought I had to prove myself with money and accomplishments. But those will always ring hollow. They will never be enough. I want to be somebody. Let me be your husband. Let me be the father of your child—of *all* your children. I got more satisfaction from striking Clermont than I did from any success I found in business."

She pulled back from him. "You struck Clermont?"

"Twice. And—that reminds me—I blackmailed him into promising to send your child to Eton." Hugo tightened his grip around her. "I've never pretended to be a good man, you know. It's just that...I'm yours." He leaned his head against hers.

Her breath was warm against his face. "Did you hit him *hard?*"

"I'm afraid I did."

"That's my Hugo." There was a grim satisfaction in her voice. "I love you, you know. If you hadn't come, as soon as winter set in and the ground became too hard to work, I'd planned to come for you."

"Well, I'm glad I came to my senses," Hugo said. "You shouldn't have traveled, not in your condition. Yet curiosity impels me to inquire. What did you plan to do, once you arrived?"

"Allow me to demonstrate." She lifted her face to his, traced the line of his jaw with her fingers. "This." She pressed a kiss to the corner of his mouth. "And this." She kissed the other corner. "And..." She took his mouth full on, her lips soft against his, tasting of all the things he'd most wanted.

"I'd do that," she whispered, "until you were forced to admit you loved me."

"I love you."

"Well, that's no fun." She kissed him again. "Now what excuse do I have?"

He drew in a shuddering breath and pulled her closer. "You could make me say it again," he whispered. "Make me say it always. Make me say it so often that you never have cause to doubt. I love you."

Aftermaths & Beginnings

Eton, not quite twelve years later.

"'PEACE SHALL GO SLEEP with Turks and infidels, and in this seat of peace tumultuous wars shall kin with kin and kind with kind confound…'"

Robert Blaisdell, the Marquess of Waring and also the eleven-year-old heir to the Duke of Clermont, looked up from his seat at the window. Sebastian Malheur, his cousin, paused in the midst of reading his lesson in Shakespeare aloud.

The other boy frowned at his book. "What does *tumultuous* mean?"

What flashed through Robert's head was not a definition, but a series of noises: the sound of china crashing against a wall; his father's shouts, the words rendered indistinct through the walls, but the intent still clear. *Tumultuous* meant the slam of a door and the quiet sound of his mother's sobs. But most of all, it was the long silence that followed: the servants not daring to draw attention to themselves by speaking, and Robert, holding his breath, hoping that maybe if he was very quiet and very good, it might not happen again.

"Tumultuous," he said, "means broken to bits."

Sebastian wrinkled his nose. "That doesn't make any sense. How can a war be broken into pieces?"

Robert was saved from answering by a shout in the yard below, and then a great clamor. The other boys who were studying in this upstairs library—all four of them—were only too happy to leave their books and press their noses to the windows that overlooked the fracas.

A crowd was forming on the green below: a mix of boys of all ages gathering in a circle around one child. While Robert watched, an older boy grabbed the child by the collar; another hit him.

"Someone should stop that," Sebastian said next to him.

Someone was going to have to be Robert. He usually did put a stop to these rows; it was what a knight-errant would do. And while Robert would never admit it to the other boys, he still fancied himself one.

"Who is it?" Sebastian added, peering down at the crowd. "Is he new?"

"Yes. He's a first form lag," someone else said. "A Colleger."

"Ah," one of the older boys said. "A scholarship student. No wonder. Who are his parents?"

"Some kind of farmers. Or soap-makers."

A derisive noise came at that. But Robert brushed his hands and stood up. Knights protected the weak, after all.

"Even worse," the older boy was saying. "Davenant asked the boy who his father was, and he said, 'Hugo Marshall.' When Davenant said he'd never heard of him, the little lag said, 'It doesn't matter; he's a better man than your sire, anyway.'"

Robert froze.

Sebastian hadn't moved from the window, but the other boy snorted. "He's got stones, that's for sure. Not so clear on the brains, unfortunately."

Robert's own brain fogged over. He set his fingertips against the glass and peered down once more. "Who did you say his father was again?"

"Hugo Marshall."

Robert had heard that name before. He had heard it a few years ago, after another awful round of arguments ended in vicious separation. That time, it had been his mother who had left the house in a slamming of doors and a pointed ordering of carriages; his father had stayed morosely behind in the study.

Robert had tiptoed into the room, and, gathering up all his courage, he'd spoken. "Father, why is Mother always sad?"

Sad wasn't the right word, but at the time he hadn't yet learned *tumultuous.*

His father had tipped back his glass of spirits and stared at the ceiling. "It's Hugo Marshall's fault," he'd said after a while. "It's all Hugo Marshall's fault."

Robert hadn't known what to make of that. What he'd finally ventured was: "Is Hugo Marshall a villain?"

"Yes," his father had said with a bitter laugh. "He's a villain. A knave. A cur. A right bloody bastard."

That *right bloody bastard* had a son, and at the moment, that son was surrounded by other boys. In the upstairs room, his friends all turned to Robert. The library seemed too small, the air too hot.

"Never say you know who this Hugo Marshall is," the older boy said.

"I have no idea." It was the first time in a very long time that Robert had told a lie. "I've never heard of him," he added swiftly, hoping the burn of his cheeks wouldn't give him away.

On fine summer days after his talk with his father, Robert had wandered in the paddocks outside, wielding a switch instead of a sword, and challenging white-headed daisies to duels. Sometimes, he imagined himself fighting dragons. But usually, he fought villains—villains and knaves and curs, all named Hugo Marshall. When he defeated him—and Sir Robert always defeated his villains—he brought the right bloody bastard home, trembling and bound, and laid the cur at his mother's feet.

After that, they all lived happily ever after. No more shouts. No more silences. No more separations.

"Do we stop it?" Sebastian asked.

Three boys turned to look at Robert. Possibly, Robert conceded, they might have looked to him because he was the only duke's heir at Eton. Maybe it had to do with the clear, blue eyes he'd inherited from his father— eyes that he'd learned made other boys nervous, if he simply stared. But the most likely reason they looked to Robert—or so he told himself—was that they sensed he was innately a knight, and therefore superior in morals and worthy of following.

"No," he said. "We encourage it. The little lag thinks he's superior to us. When he's drummed out, he'll know better."

Beside him, Sebastian frowned in puzzlement.

Robert turned away sharply. "You don't have any questions, Malheur, do you?"

"No," his cousin said after a long pause. "None at all."

⌘ ⌘ ⌘

ROBERT MADE IT A POINT to avoid Marshall for as long as he could. It wasn't hard—he'd been attending Eton for quite a while now, and the other boy was just starting. Normally, a new boy who arrived might go through the usual rounds of roughhousing, while everyone figured out where he stood. Once he found his place in the pecking order, he might keep it with a minimum of fuss and scarcely a blackened eye.

But Marshall had no place at Eton. Robert was determined that this would be the case. He chanced to remark on the boy's jacket, and someone cracked an egg on it. He made a comment about how amusing it would be if a soap-seller's son had to bathe in slops, and Marshall's soap was replaced with bars of mud.

He had never expected Marshall to recognize that Robert was the instigator of his problems. He was even more surprised when the boy started to fight back like the ill-mannered cur that he was. Marshall began to construct snide insults in Latin—clever enough that the other boys sniggered about them. And after that incident with the mud, *someone* crept into Robert's room and stole all his undergarments. He found them in the larder, stuffed into a barrel of pickles—wet, cold, and salty. No amount of laundering could remove the smell of vinegar.

Some things were not to be borne. That was when Robert knew he was going to have to confront the boy directly.

He found his quarry against the far stone wall of the cricket field. He wasn't the first to have at him; by the time he got there, the boy had his back against the wall. He'd set his spectacles a few feet behind him, and he held his fists in the air.

"Come on, you cowards," Marshall was saying. "Three-on-one not good enough odds for you?" It was the first time that Robert had seen Marshall this close. His hair was a thin, light orange; his skin was pale and freckled. His eye was ringed with a virulent red bruise; it would be purple in the morning. He spat pink and turned lightly on his feet, facing his attackers. That was when the boy caught sight of Robert.

"Speaking of cowards," he said.

"I'm no coward." Robert rolled up his sleeves and stepped forward. "Call me a coward again—I dare you. Don't you know who I am?"

Everyone else stepped back, giving the two of them a wide berth. Robert circled the other boy, holding his fists up. And that was when he noticed something curious. Marshall's eyes were blue—an icy blue.

A *familiar* icy blue. Robert saw eyes like that in the mirror every day.

"I know who you are," Marshall said with disdain. "You're my brother."

Robert had always thought it a ridiculous thing to say in stories—that someone's world turned upside down. But there was no other way to describe what happened. The other boy's words hit with the force of a cannonball, crashing through everything he'd known.

"You can't be my brother."

But he recalled too clearly the crash of china, his mother's shouts. *Philanderer! Whoreson!*

Philanderer. Marshall had Robert's eyes. He had his father's eyes.

Marshall sniffed and wiped at his nose. "Don't your parents tell you anything?"

"No!" He wasn't sure if it was an answer or a denial. And the other boy said that with such a matter-of-fact air—as if *his* parents were a single unit, who might sit a boy down and have a conversation with him.

Robert's head was whirling. "How can you be my brother if your father is Hugo Marshall?"

The other boy spat once again and didn't answer.

He didn't have to. Robert had only the faintest notion of what *philandering* entailed—gambling and drinking and getting wenches with child.

He'd never given much thought to the possibility that wenches who were gotten with child ended up having them.

The other boy simply shrugged all this away.

Five hundred days playing alone in the paddock, and he had a *brother?* It was not just his mother and father who were broken to bits. He was, too. Robert thought of soap turned to mud, of fights, of Marshall's eye—which would be black by morning.

He thought of the three boys who had been fighting him when Robert arrived. They'd done that ungentlemanly thing because Robert had encouraged it.

Even if this boy wasn't his brother, *Robert* was the villain in this piece. And if what Marshall said was true…

Robert was the knave, the cur, the right bloody bastard. Nothing would ever end happily ever after again. Not unless—

Some decisions were not difficult at all. "Hit me," he said urgently, low enough that the other boys couldn't hear. "Hit me hard. Knock me down."

Marshall didn't even hesitate. He stepped forward and smashed his fist against Robert's nose. Robert didn't need to pretend to fall; his legs crumpled of their own accord. When he picked himself off the ground, his nose was running red. He swiped the blood away and pushed himself to his feet.

"Did you really not know?" Marshall asked him.

He'd hit with his left hand.

"Can you hit harder with your right?" Robert asked.

Marshall's chin went up. "I can hit hard enough with both."

"Because I'm left-handed, too. You've just knocked me down, and I've acknowledged it. They shouldn't bother you anymore. Not after that." He was babbling. He gingerly extended his hand—his left hand. "Pax?"

The other boy stared at him for a moment. Then, finally, he extended his own left hand. "Pax," he agreed. "But you break the peace, and I'll break you."

"Well," Sebastian said, coming up from behind them. "This is going to be interesting."

Thank you!

Thanks for reading *The Governess Affair*. I hope you enjoyed it!

- Would you like to know when my next book is available? You can sign up for my new release e-mail list at www.courtneymilan.com, follow me on twitter at @courtneymilan, or like my Facebook page at http://facebook.com/courtneymilanauthor.
- Reviews help other readers find books. I appreciate all reviews, whether positive or negative.
- You've just read the prequel to the Brothers Sinister series. The other books in the series are *The Duchess War*, *A Kiss for Midwinter*, *The Heiress Effect*, *The Countess Conspiracy* (out December 2013), and *The Mistress Rebellion* (out sometime in 2014). I hope you enjoy them all!

If you'd like to read the first chapter of *The Duchess War*, the first full-length book in the Brothers Sinister series, please turn the page.

The Duchess War: Excerpt

The Brothers Sinister series is about the next generation: Hugo and Serena's son Oliver, and his unlikely friendship with his half-brother, Robert Blaisdell, the son of the new Duke of Clermont.

The Duchess War *is the first full-length book in the series.*

Miss Minerva Lane is a quiet, bespectacled wallflower, and she wants to keep it that way. After all, the last time she was the center of attention, it ended badly—so badly that she changed her name to escape her scandalous past. Wallflowers may not be the prettiest of blooms, but at least they don't get trampled. So when a handsome duke comes to town, the last thing she wants is his attention.

But that is precisely what she gets…

Chapter One

ROBERT BLAISDELL, THE NINTH DUKE OF CLERMONT, was not hiding.

True, he'd retreated to the upstairs library of the old Guildhall, far enough from the crowd below that the noise of the ensemble had faded to a distant rumble. True, nobody else was about. Also true: He stood behind thick curtains of blue-gray velvet, which shielded him from view. And he'd had to move the heavy davenport of brown-buttoned leather to get there.

But he'd done all that not to hide himself, but because—and this was a key point in his rather specious train of logic—in this centuries-old structure of plaster and timberwork, only one of the panes in the windows opened, and that happened to be the one secreted behind the sofa.

So here he stood, cigarillo in hand, the smoke trailing out into the chilly autumn air. He wasn't hiding; it was simply a matter of preserving the aging books from fumes.

He might even have believed himself, if only he smoked.

Still, through the wavy panes of aging glass, he could make out the darkened stone of the church directly across the way. Lamplight cast unmoving shadows on the pavement below. A pile of handbills had once been stacked against the doors, but an autumn breeze had picked them up and scattered them down the street, driving them into puddles.

He was making a mess. A goddamned glorious mess. He smiled and tapped the end of his untouched cigarillo against the window opening, sending ashes twirling to the paving stones below.

The quiet creak of a door opening startled him. He turned from the window at the corresponding scritch of floorboards. Someone had come up the stairs and entered the adjoining room. The footsteps were light—a woman's, perhaps, or a child's. They were also curiously hesitant. Most people who made their way to the library in the midst of a musicale had a reason to do so. A clandestine meeting, perhaps, or a search for a missing family member.

From his vantage point behind the curtains, Robert could only see a small slice of the library. Whoever it was drew closer, walking hesitantly. She was out of sight—somehow he was sure that she was a woman—but he could hear the soft, prowling fall of her feet, pausing every so often as if to examine the surroundings.

She didn't call out a name or make a determined search. It didn't sound as if she were looking for a hidden lover. Instead, her footsteps circled the perimeter of the room.

It took Robert half a minute to realize that he'd waited too long to announce himself. "Aha!" he could imagine himself proclaiming, springing out from behind the curtains. "I was admiring the plaster. Very evenly laid back there, did you know?"

She would think he was mad. And so far, nobody yet had come to that conclusion. So instead of speaking, he dropped his cigarillo out the window. It tumbled end over end, orange tip glowing, until it landed in a puddle and extinguished itself.

All he could see of the room was a half-shelf of books, the back of the sofa, and a table next to it on which a chess set had been laid out. The game was in progress; from what little he remembered of the rules, black was winning. Whoever it was drew nearer, and Robert shrank back against the window.

She crossed into his field of vision.

She wasn't one of the young ladies he'd met in the crowded hall earlier. Those had all been beauties, hoping to catch his eye. And she—whoever she was—was not a beauty. Her dark hair was swept into a no-nonsense knot at the back of her neck. Her lips were thin and her nose was sharp and a bit on the long side. She was dressed in a dark blue gown trimmed in ivory—no lace, no ribbons, just simple fabric. Even the cut of her gown bordered on the severe side: waist pulled in so tightly he wondered how she could breathe, sleeves marching from her shoulders to her wrists without an inch of excess fabric to soften the picture.

She didn't see Robert standing behind the curtain. She had set her head to one side and was eyeing the chess set the way a member of the Temperance League might look at a cask of brandy: as if it were an evil to be stamped out with prayer and song—and failing that, with martial law.

She took one halting step forward, then another. Then, she reached into the silk bag that hung around her wrist and retrieved a pair of spectacles.

Glasses should have made her look more severe. But as soon as she put them on, her gaze softened.

He'd read her wrongly. Her eyes hadn't been narrowed in scorn; she'd been squinting. It hadn't been severity he saw in her gaze but something else entirely—something he couldn't quite make out. She reached out and picked up a black knight, turning it around, over and over. He could see nothing about the pieces that would merit such careful attention. They were solid wood, carved with indifferent skill. Still, she studied it, her eyes wide and luminous.

Then, inexplicably, she raised it to her lips and kissed it.

Robert watched in frozen silence. It almost felt as if he were interrupting a tryst between a woman and her lover. This was a lady who had secrets, and she didn't want to share them.

The door in the far room creaked as it opened once more.

The woman's eyes grew wide and wild. She looked about frantically and dove over the davenport in her haste to hide, landing in an ignominious heap two feet away from him. She didn't see Robert even then; she curled into a ball, yanking her skirts behind the leather barrier of the sofa, breathing in shallow little gulps.

Good thing he'd moved the davenport back half a foot earlier. She never would have fit the great mass of her skirts behind it otherwise.

Her fist was still clenched around the chess piece; she shoved the knight violently under the sofa.

This time, a heavier pair of footfalls entered the room.

"Minnie?" said a man's voice. "Miss Pursling? Are you here?"

Her nose scrunched and she pushed back against the wall. She made no answer.

"Gad, man." Another voice that Robert didn't recognize—young and slightly slurred with drink. "I don't envy you that one."

"Don't speak ill of my almost-betrothed," the first voice said. "You know she's perfect for me."

"That timid little rodent?"

"She'll keep a good home. She'll see to my comfort. She'll manage the children, and she won't complain about my mistresses." There was a creak of hinges—the unmistakable sound of someone opening one of the glass doors that protected the bookshelves.

"What are you doing, Gardley?" the drunk man asked. "Looking for her among the German volumes? I don't think she'd fit." That came with an ugly laugh.

Gardley. That couldn't be the elder Mr. Gardley, owner of a distillery—not by the youth in that voice. This must be Mr. Gardley the younger. Robert had seen him from afar—an unremarkable fellow of medium height, medium-brown hair, and features that reminded him faintly of five other people.

"On the contrary," young Gardley said. "I think she'll fit quite well. As wives go, Miss Pursling will be just like these books. When I wish to take her down and read her, she'll be there. When I don't, she'll wait patiently, precisely where she was left. She'll make me a comfortable wife, Ames. Besides, my mother likes her."

Robert didn't believe he'd met an Ames. He shrugged and glanced down at—he was guessing—Miss Pursling to see how she took this revelation.

She didn't look surprised or shocked at her almost-fiancé's unromantic utterance. Instead, she looked resigned.

"You'll have to take her to bed, you know," Ames said.

"True. But not, thank God, very often."

"She's a rodent. Like all rodents, I imagine she'll squeal when she's poked."

There was a mild thump.

"What?" yelped Ames.

"That," said Gardley, "is my future wife you are talking about."

Maybe the fellow wasn't so bad after all.

Then Gardley continued. "I'm the only one who gets to think about poking *that* rodent."

Miss Pursling pressed her lips together and looked up, as if imploring the heavens. But inside the library, there were no heavens to implore. And when she looked up, through the gap in the curtains…

Her gaze met Robert's. Her eyes grew big and round. She didn't scream; she didn't gasp. She didn't twitch so much as an inch. She simply fixed him with a look that bristled with silent, venomous accusation. Her nostrils flared.

There was nothing Robert could do but lift his hand and give her a little wave.

She took off her spectacles and turned away in a gesture so regally dismissive that he had to look twice to remind himself that she was, in fact, sitting in a heap of skirts at his feet. That from this awkward angle above her, he could see straight down the neckline of her gown—right at the one part of her figure that didn't strike him as severe, but soft—

Save that for later, he admonished himself, and adjusted his gaze up a few inches. Because she'd turned away, he saw for the first time a faint scar on her left cheek, a tangled white spider web of crisscrossed lines.

"Wherever your mouse has wandered off to, it's not here," Ames was saying. "Likely she's in the lady's retiring room. I say we go back to the fun. You can always tell your mother you had words with her in the library."

"True enough," Gardley said. "And I don't need to mention that she wasn't present for them—it's not as if she would have said anything in response, even if she had been here."

Footsteps receded; the door creaked once more, and the men walked out.

Miss Pursling didn't look at Robert once they'd left, not even to acknowledge his existence with a glare. Instead, she pushed herself to her knees, made a fist, and slammed it into the hard back of the sofa—once, then twice, hitting it so hard that it moved forward with the force of her blow—all one hundred pounds of it.

He caught her wrist before she landed a third strike. "There now," he said. "You don't want to hurt yourself over him. He doesn't deserve it."

She stared up at him, her eyes wide.

He didn't see how any man could call this woman timid. She positively crackled with defiance. He let go of her arm before the fury in her could travel up his hand and consume him. He had enough anger of his own.

"Never mind me," she said. "Apparently I'm not capable of helping myself."

He almost jumped. He wasn't sure how he'd expected her voice to sound—sharp and severe, like her appearance suggested? Perhaps he'd imagined her talking in a high squeak, as if she were the rodent she'd been labeled. But her voice was low, warm, and deeply sensual. It was the kind of voice that made him suddenly aware that she was on her knees before him, her head almost level with his crotch.

Save that for later, too.

"I'm a rodent. All rodents squeal when poked." She punched the sofa once again. She was going to bruise her knuckles if she kept that up. "Are you planning to poke me, too?"

"No." Stray thoughts didn't count, thank God; if they did, all men would burn in hell forever.

"Do you always skulk behind curtains, hoping to overhear intimate conversations?"

Robert felt the tips of his ears burn. "Do you always leap behind sofas when you hear your fiancé coming?"

"Yes," she said defiantly. "Didn't you hear? I'm like a book that has been mislaid. One day, one of his servants will find me covered in dust in the middle of spring-cleaning. 'Ah,' the butler will say. 'That's where Miss Wilhelmina has ended up. I had forgotten all about her.'"

Wilhelmina Pursling? What a dreadful appellation.

She took a deep breath. "Please don't tell anyone. Not about any of this." She shut her eyes and pressed her fingers to her eyes. "Please just go away, whoever you are."

He brushed the curtains to one side and made his way around the sofa. From a few feet away, he couldn't even see her. He could only imagine her curled on the floor, furious to the point of tears.

"Minnie," he said. It wasn't polite to call her by so intimate a name. And yet he wanted to hear it on his tongue.

She didn't respond.

"I'll give you twenty minutes," he said. "If I don't see you downstairs by then, I'll come up for you."

For a few moments, there was no answer. Then: "The beautiful thing about marriage is the right it gives me to monogamy. One man intent on dictating my whereabouts is enough, wouldn't you think?"

He stared at the sofa in confusion before he realized that she thought he'd been threatening to drag her out.

Robert was good at many things. Communicating with women was not one of them.

"That's not what I meant," he muttered. "It's just…" He walked back to the sofa and peered over the leather top. "If a woman I cared about was hiding behind a sofa, I would hope that someone would take the time to make sure she was well."

There was a long pause. Then fabric rustled and she looked up at him. Her hair had begun to slip out of that severe bun; it hung around her face, softening her features, highlighting the pale whiteness of her scar. Not pretty, but…interesting. And he could have listened to her talk all night.

She stared at him in puzzlement. "Oh," she said flatly. "You're attempting to be kind." She sounded as if the possibility had never occurred to her before. She let out a sigh, and gave him a shake of her head. "But your kindness is misplaced. You see, *that*—" she pointed toward the doorway where her near-fiancé had disappeared "—that is the best possible outcome I can hope for. I have wanted just such a thing for years. As soon as I can stomach the thought, I'll be marrying him."

There was no trace of sarcasm in her voice. She stood. With a practiced hand, she smoothed her hair back under the pins and straightened her skirts until she was restored to complete propriety.

Only then did she stoop, patting under the sofa to find where she'd tossed the knight. She examined the chessboard, cocked her head, and then very, very carefully, set the piece back into place.

While he was standing there, watching her, trying to make sense of her words, she walked out the door.

Want to read the rest? *The Duchess War* is available now.

Other Books by Courtney

Acknowledgements

THERE ARE ALWAYS MORE people to thank than I can remember. As always, Tessa Dare, Carey Baldwin, and Leigh LaValle provided emotional support and help in the writing of this novella. The Northwest Pixies (plus additional friends) helped shame me into making sure I met my word count goals, with special mentions to Rachel Grant (for the magic coffee mug), and Darcy Burke and Natasha Tate for talking me through some parts of the middle.

I'm always grateful for my amazing team: Robin Harders and Martha Trachtenberg for editing, and Christine Dixon and Tina Marie for proofreading, and to Kristin Nelson and Lori Bennett who are helping me reach even more readers.

And then there are all those who provided support in so many ways— my husband and family, my dog and cat (yes, even the cat); the Pixies; the Loop That Must Not be Named.

Most of all, thanks to all my readers. Your support and enthusiasm mean everything to me.

Made in the USA
San Bernardino, CA
31 March 2017